S

Forthcoming titles by Dora Heldt:
Inseparable
Vacation with Dad
Aunt Inge's Secret Escape

Life after Forty

DORA HELDT

TRANSLATED BY Jamie Lee Searle

PUBLISHED BY

amazoncrossing

Text copyright © 2006 Deutscher Taschenbuch Verlag GmbH & Co. KG
English translation copyright © 2011 Amazon Content Services
All rights reserved.
Printed in the United States of America.

Life After Forty was first published in 2006 by Deutscher Taschenbuch Verlag GmbH & Co. KG as *Ausgeliebt*. Translated from German by Jamie Lee Searle. Published in English by AmazonCrossing in 2011.

Published by AmazonCrossing
P.O. Box 400818
Las Vegas, NV 89140

ISBN-13: 978-1439279632
ISBN-10: 1439279632
Library of Congress Control Number: 2010918699

The Phone Call

Just as Hugh Grant was jumping into the car to rush to the airport and intercept the love of his life at the very last moment, the telephone rang. My sister and I both sighed.

"Oh, but it's only ten minutes from the end."

Ines pressed the pause button, stood up, and picked up the phone. I looked at Hugh Grant, desperately in love and caught on freeze frame.

"It's for you. Your husband must be missing you."

"Oh nonsense, I only left this morning."

We lived in the countryside, about 150 kilometers from Hamburg. On the North Sea coast, right by the sea and at the end of the world, or that's how it felt anyway. It was beautiful there. Bernd had grown up in the village, but it admittedly wasn't a great base for my job. I frequently visited clients in Hamburg and Niedersachsen and often had to stay overnight. Whenever I had appointments in Hamburg, I stayed with my sister. This was my first evening at her place, and we had planned a lazy girls' night in, complete with *Notting Hill* and chilled white wine.

My husband wasn't the type for pining, even though I often hoped that could change. I took the phone from Ines.

"So, Bernd, what did I forget? Can I call you back in bit? Our film's only ten minutes from the end."

"I have to talk to you."

Something in his voice made me leave where I was sitting next to my sister and take the phone into her office.

"What about?"

Bernd cleared his throat and fell silent. So did I.

We had been married for almost ten years. In the last four, something had changed between us. For the most part I just suppressed my thoughts and hoped things would improve. Bernd wasn't the kind of man who found it easy to speak about his feelings, and he would bring any conversation I started about us to an abrupt end. So I'd just reconciled myself to being part of a good team. After all, you can't really expect to still have the same emotional intensity and passionate sex after ten years together.

The silence was broken by Bernd clearing his throat again. I couldn't bear it anymore.

"Has something happened?"

"Yes…no, I mean, I've been thinking."

It seemed like he was drunk.

"What about?"

"I…um, well, Christine, I want a divorce."

It hit me like a thunderbolt. I suddenly felt sick and could feel my heart racing. I started to shake. I had the feeling I didn't have much time.

"Have you been drinking? What's happened? Is something wrong? I mean…everything was fine this morning. What does all this mean? Bernd, say something, will you!"

My voice had become shrill. Bernd cleared his throat again, but said nothing.

I couldn't understand what was happening. Over the weekend everything had been as normal. On Saturday we'd been to a party at our neighbors' place; it was a nice evening, and everyone had been in a good mood. Bernd had gone home relatively early and told me to stay on. He said he'd just drunk a little too much wine and was feeling tired.

When I got back later, he was already in bed, asleep.

Sunday was just like countless Sundays that had gone before it. We had breakfast, and then I worked at my desk while Bernd repaired something or other in the garage. We went to his parents' for lunch and spent the afternoon reading, drinking coffee, watching TV, and ironing. In the evening I packed my bag for the week ahead. Everything was as normal.

And now, just twenty-four hours later, this.

"Bernd, please, you can't just ring me up at Ines's and spring something like this on me."

"It's just that everything's gotten to be too much for me—the house, my job, our marriage. Life's too short."

I didn't understand.

"What's wrong with the house? Why don't we see if we can change something then? We'll figure something out together."

"It's not about that. I just don't want to live with you anymore."

I felt sick to my stomach.

"But we have to talk properly. I mean, we can't just discuss this on the phone."

"When will you be back?"

My travel schedule, with all my appointments on it, had been hanging in the kitchen for years. But despite that Bernd never knew where I was or when.

"I'll rearrange my appointments somehow. I'll be back tomorrow evening."

"Okay, we'll talk then. But it won't change my decision."

At that moment I suddenly realized what he meant and what was happening. My entire body felt alien to me, as if it belonged to someone else.

"Till tomorrow then."

He'd already hung up.

I pressed the red button and laid the phone carefully down on the desk. Then I went slowly back into the living room.

"About time, too. Surely that could've waited until we finished the film?"

Ines put her book down and reached for the remote. Then she looked at me.

"For God's sake, Christine, what's happened?"

I looked at Hugh Grant, still desperately in love, then at Ines's worried face.

"Bernd wants a divorce. Life's too short, apparently."

And then came the tears. And the brutal pain.

The Plan

Three hours later I'd calmed down enough to be able to string coherent sentences together.

Ines was a trained children's nurse and used to dealing with hysterical little children. The experience came in handy for older sisters too. To be on the safe side, she fixed me a cup of tea with rum. I told her about the last few years of my marriage. Bernd's indifference, his increasing unreliability, my unhappiness, his refusal to talk things over, his eternal moaning about the stress of his job. Everything was in a rut. We never had arguments; we were always nice to one another. I just wasn't allowed to complain about anything.

I talked and cried and talked.

And last but not least, the painful fact that Bernd would only sleep with me nowadays if he was drunk.

Ines listened to me with a concentrated look on her face, passed me tissues, lit cigarettes, poured me more tea and rum, and just let me talk. Finally, completely exhausted and a little drunk, I had to pause for breath, and she spoke.

"It sounds to me as though there's another woman involved."

I flinched, but shook my head. Bernd had become so idle and passionless of late that I didn't think he was even capable of making the effort.

"I would have noticed something."

"If you'd wanted to. I just can't bring myself to believe that your lethargic and unorganized husband, who's still predominantly living off of your income, would prefer to live without you than with you. After all, he was always able to do whatever he wanted, and he's never shown consideration for anyone but himself. It's not like you've ever complained about anything, so what would the advantages be? I certainly can't think of any. Quite the reverse in fact."

I felt the need to defend him. But I couldn't think of anything to say.

Ines took her hand from my shoulder and sat down. She was one of those people who are deeply convinced that all crises and problems are best solved with the help of lists and tables. By putting down thoughts, plans, and ideas on paper and working through them one by one.

"Try to think clearly now. What's going to happen when you talk tomorrow evening?"

She already had a pen in her hand.

"Do you want to fight for your marriage?"

The notepad was now on the table.

"What can I say to someone who doesn't want to live with me anymore? Try to convince him that I'm not that awful after all? After ten years?"

Ines crossed through the words "Keep going" on the notepad.

"Okay. So you'll make a fresh start."

She underlined the words. Then started writing numbers.

"Where do you want to go?"

"I'll move to Hamburg."

"Are you sure?"

Ines wrote "Relocation to Hamburg" next to point one.

"I can't live in that house out in the sticks by myself. I only did it for Bernd's sake. What would I do there all by myself? Everything's gone downhill since we bought the damn place."

My tears started to flow again.

"Then we'll look for an apartment for you here. A really chic one. You know the area, you've got colleagues and friends here, and you can finally get out of that backwater."

Names were appearing next to point two: Dorothea, Georg, Leonie, Jörg, Nina, Franziska.

I blew my nose and tried to calm down. Just seeing the names helped. It would be nice to be able to spontaneously arrange to see them, to not have to plan to stay overnight every time. They had very rarely come to visit us out in the country. Bernd wasn't exactly an expert at hiding his dislike of visits from people who weren't really *his* friends. Leonie had visited us once; she'd gone for a walk on the beach with her husband and then come by the house afterwards. Bernd had just stared fixedly at their sandy shoes and hadn't said a single word to them. As soon as they were out of the door, he started vacuuming. Unfortunately, they turned back before getting to the car because Leonie had forgotten her shawl. Bernd had opened the door with the vacuum in his hand. It was their first and last visit.

Suddenly another name came to mind, and the tears started to flow again.

"What about Antje?"

Ines was already writing point three.

"Antje. Listen, you've been friends for twenty-five years now, fifteen of which you've spent living in different towns. You've always managed before."

Antje was my oldest and best friend. After her divorce a few years ago, I had convinced her to move from Hamburg nearer to me. She and her two children, my goddaughters. We now lived just five kilometers apart. I would be leaving her in the lurch.

A wave of sorrow rushed through my body.

I would have to leave my cats behind too. I didn't know a dentist in Hamburg, or a mechanic, or a baker. All my familiar routes would be gone. I'd never spend Christmas with Bernd again, would never again have breakfast together on Sundays or birthdays. And what would my parents say?

Ines watched me and tried to make sense of my tear-constricted stammers. She managed to decipher the word "parents," and under point three she wrote "Sylt."

"You'll be able to get back home much quicker from Hamburg than from your old place. At least two hours quicker."

Bernd hated Sylt. My parents still lived there, and we could have visited them much more often, but he always said the journey was too long. So I didn't go very often and was often homesick as a result.

I gradually started to calm down again. Realizing it was already half past three in the morning, I started to feel guilty. Ines had to be in the clinic in four hours time. She looked very tired and was yawning. I pulled myself together.

"Come on, let's go to bed. I didn't realize how late it was."

"It doesn't matter. Okay then, try to sleep and wake me up if you need me."

She stroked my cheek, making my eyes fill with tears again, and went to bed.

The last few hours of the night were filled with the same pictures running through my mind, over and over. Bernd, suntanned, when I first met him, the two of us on the beach, at parties, in the yard, in Portugal on vacation, his face in the morning, at lunchtime, in the evening. As the tears fell relentlessly down my face, I felt utterly convinced that I had just lost the love of my life.

The Hurt

A few hours later, I felt numb as I made my way to my first appointment.

My clients were booksellers. They ordered the latest books produced by various publishing houses from me to sell to their customers. I had known them all for years and hoped that no one would notice that my world had just been turned upside down. I wouldn't be able to handle their pity.

But it seemed that no one noticed a thing. Or at least, they didn't mention it to me. I managed to get through my scheduled appointments on autopilot and just hoped that I'd make it through the day. It was only on my journey back that the sadness washed over me again. My fear of the conversation looming before me was breaking through the numbness.

As I drove into the driveway, it seemed almost strange that everything looked just as it had when I'd left. My cats came over to greet me, the mailbox was full, and my neighbor waved at me. Everything was just like it always was. Bernd had seen me from the window and opened the front door. That was different. He cleared his throat, gave a subdued smile, and took my bag from me, a gesture which seemed to surprise even him.

"So, how was it?"

I couldn't think of an answer. Not to do justice to the night and day I'd just had.

"Um, have you eaten anything? Would you like a cup of coffee?"

Everything felt wrong.

"I'm not hungry. I just want to talk."

I sat down at the kitchen table. Bernd began to feed the cats. I watched him for a while.

"Bernd, please, fill up the bowls properly!"

He went to the sink and scrubbed the water bowl. With the brush we used for the dishes.

I could feel a crashing headache coming on, and my skin felt itchy. With great effort, I concentrated on not losing my temper. Finally, he sat down on the chair next to me. Then he stood straight back up, fetched an ashtray and his cigarettes, and then sat back down again. I looked at him. He looked the same as he always had.

"So?"

"What more is there to say? I already told you everything yesterday."

"On the phone. At Ines's. Why didn't you do it on the weekend?"

"It's easier by phone. And it was good that you weren't alone."

I had to take a deep breath. What a thing to say. *Easier.*

"Can you at least explain why?"

"I already have."

"But I don't understand."

I breathed deeply again and thought about my conversation with Ines.

"Have you met someone else?"

"Nonsense, when would I have met someone? It's about me. It's not your fault."

"I don't believe you. Something must have happened."

"Let it go; nothing's happened."

He stood up, fetched two mugs from the cupboard, and poured the coffee.

"So, you can stay here, of course; I'll move out."

"I won't be able to manage it, not the house and the yard and the cats. Not with my job. I'll probably move to Hamburg."

I watched him. Perhaps he would realize what we were doing.

"Yes, you should do that. After all, Hamburg is a great place and so practical for you. I'll help you with the move, of course."

I felt sick. I couldn't understand what was happening, just that it *was* happening. We sat in the kitchen a while longer. I battled to stop my tears and the questions pouring out. Bernd avoided giving proper answers and just spouted sentences like "We'll stay friends," and "There's no need to legalize the divorce right away, not with the current tax rates."

After a while I couldn't bear it anymore and went upstairs. As I lay down on the bed, unable to hold the tears back any longer, I heard the front door slam shut and then Bernd's car starting up.

An hour later I didn't have the strength left to cry anymore. I felt abandoned, humiliated, and very alone. I thought of calling Ines, but I didn't want to unload on her again so soon. Then I thought of Antje; she'd have to know sooner or later in any case. I dialed her number. After the second ring I heard her voice.

"Antje, it's me. Bernd wants a divorce."

The tears were back again.

"What? Oh, you poor thing. What a shame, but then I always did think you'd end up separating from him."

"I didn't want to. Antje, I'll probably move to Hamburg. I don't want to stay here alone. But what about you?"

"Don't you worry about me. If it weren't for the children, then I would have stayed in the city too; it's what you should do. And it's not the first divorce that we'll get through together. I'll help you; we'll figure it all out."

We spoke for a few more minutes. After I hung up, I felt a little comforted. Then I phoned Marleen. She was the ex-wife of Bernd's best friend. We'd met each other through our husbands, lived in the same town, and had become close in recent years. Besides that, she was refreshingly robust and practical; I had no reason to fear pity from her. After my short explanation, she asked the reason for the separation, found my answer unsatisfactory, and offered me her guest room. I politely refused, but promised to call her again over the next few days.

The next few days and weeks passed as though everything was covered in dense fog. Parts of my life were reassuringly normal: I visited my booksellers, kept my appointments as planned, and made no mention whatsoever of what was currently going on in my life. On one of the evenings that I spent with Ines, Leonie came by. Ines had met up with her and told her everything. We had been colleagues for a number of years, and we saw each other three or four times a year outside of work.

Standing in front of the door with a bottle of champagne, she didn't beat around the bush.

"It's all good: I still have a picture of him in my mind standing there with that vacuum in his hand, he wasn't interested in your job, he never read any books, and he never came to Hamburg. Just be happy that you're rid of him and can get out of that backwater. Here's to the start of your new life!"

I didn't yet share her opinion, but I was touched when she—by herself and together with Ines—viewed numerous apartments over the following weeks, whittled them down to possibles, and arranged three or four viewings for me over the weekends. When I wasn't looking at apartments, I went to visit my parents in Sylt, spent hours running along the beach in the March cold, cried a little, and slept a lot.

Once a week I had to go back to the house. It was still my address for my office, and all my mail was sent there. Bernd kept out of my way. If he was at home, I went to see Marleen, who had already arranged for moving boxes and a map of Hamburg for me. She had put her divorce behind her, and I found her unshakeable optimism very comforting.

"Sweetheart, trust me, in six months' time you'll look back and laugh at it all."

By now, everyone knew. Lots of people avoided me, which I found hurtful. Perhaps they thought separations could be contagious. I hadn't heard much from Antje either. It occurred to me when Marleen asked after her one evening as we were sitting in her kitchen. It was the beginning of April. Ines and Leonie had found an apartment for me, which I'd managed to secure. Nine hundred square feet, terrace, open fireplace, and a balcony leading off of the kitchen. It was situated almost exactly between Ines and Leonie, a fifteen-minute drive from them both. This made my heart feel a lot lighter, and so Marleen's question didn't bother me too much.

"Antje is so busy. Children, a job—you know what it's like. She's helping me with the move. She already booked the fifteenth off work."

"I just find it a bit strange. She's your best friend, and yet you haven't heard from her in six weeks. Does she even know that you've found an apartment?"

"I'll tell her tomorrow. I'm going over there for Karola's birthday. And Marleen, I know you're not particularly fond of Antje, but you just don't know her that well, that's all."

She didn't answer. I had the feeling that she wanted to tell me something. But I didn't ask, and she said nothing more.

When I went out to the car the next day with a birthday present in my hand, Bernd followed me.

"Where are you off to?"

"It's Karola's birthday. She's ten today."

"Do you have time to be going to a child's birthday party? I thought you wanted to pack."

"She's my goddaughter. I'll manage the packing in time; I've still got two weeks."

"Well, you know best, I guess."

Bernd turned around and went back into the house. Maybe he was regretting his decision after all. I didn't understand what had put him in such a bad mood; he usually seemed very happy not to have to see me in the house.

When I rang Antje's doorbell, Karola opened the door and flung herself around my neck.

"You're here at last! Are you better now? Is that for me? Can I open it now?"

Answers weren't necessary; the hallway was suddenly full of ten-year-old girls all shouting at once. I squeezed past them and went into the kitchen. Antje was standing in front of the stove and stirring a pot with a concentrated expression. She only raised her head briefly to nod at me.

"Hi, Christina, how's it going?"

Then she buried her head back in the recipe next to her. I was amazed.

"Hi, Antje. You know, nothing new. What's up with you?"

"Oh, you know what it's like. These birthday parties always stress me out. I spent the whole afternoon running around town, my feet are sore, and Kathleen, that friend of Karola's, the fat one, she's got one heck of a voice on her."

She was chattering like a wind-up puppet, loud, banal sentences, not looking up at me even once. I went over to her and pushed the recipe away.

"Have I done something to upset you?"

"No, er, it's just…nothing. So, it's really great that you've got a terrace in your new place. That means you can take the wicker beach chair with you."

I suddenly went cold. First it was just a feeling, and then my brain started to work. She stared into the pot.

"Antje?"

She was silent, just stirring.

I took my bag and my jacket and went into the children's room to say goodbye to Karola. She was caught up with unwrapping her presents, smiling at her friends with her eyes sparkling.

I left.

The Beginning

nes sat on her toolbox and uncapped her beer bottle with a cigarette lighter. She looked first at Dorothea, then me, with a triumphant smile.

"Nine minutes."

Dorothea nodded at her and rubbed the blister on her forefinger.

"Under ten—I knew it."

I'd come into the living room with a box full of books and had no idea what they were talking about.

"What's nine minutes?"

Ines put the bottle to her mouth, took a few long swigs, put it down again, and then looked at me.

"That's a record. We just built the last Billy bookcase in under ten minutes."

Dorothea held up her forefinger for me to see.

"Under ten. With this blister!"

Years ago she'd been my brother Georg's girlfriend. After a while their love had faded, but the friendship had stayed. And Dorothea, who had won our family's hearts with her charm and wit, stayed too. She was very enthusiastic about my plan to move to Hamburg. She lived there as well.

Ines put her lighter against another bottle of beer, opened it, and handed it to Dorothea. She pushed herself off from the wall, took a chair from where it was stacked, upturned against another, and sat down with a groan.

"My back! And this blister. And you think I can drink after eight Billys?"

"After eight Billys, it's compulsory to have a drink. Want one too, Christine?"

I looked around me. Everything was all over the place. Empty bookshelves, coats, cushions, and curtains all over the sofa, chairs stacked on top of one another, rolls of carpet and moving boxes everywhere.

"It's getting worse and worse in here."

My heart sank.

"Well, Christine, I really think you could at least tidy up a little. You used to be so neat, and as soon as you're in the big city, then bam—you let it all go!"

Dorothea laughed heartily at her own joke. She tapped the bookshelf that was serving as a table, full of beer bottles, bags of licorice, cigarette ashes, bottle caps, and various screws.

"I mean, at least put a tablecloth down; then it'll have some style around here."

Ines laughed too.

"And I'm sure you've got some coasters for the bottles. Not that we're making rings."

Dorothea wanted to say more, but she was laughing so hard she was crying.

"You're silly."

Ines shook her head with amusement and handed me a beer.

"She's just exhausted. These artistic types aren't used to hard work."

Dorothea was a costume designer; she worked in television and also painted. Sweeping her dark locks and the tears from her face with the backs of her hands, she put on a hurt expression.

"Eight Billys, three of which I did with a blister. Not to mention the chest of drawers, desk, and kitchen table."

"The kitchen table came ready-made!"

"Well, I put a tablecloth on it at least."

She roared with laughter again.

Her silliness was catching. We sat for a while amongst the boxes of books just giggling and drinking beer. Eventually Ines got up, dropped the empty bottles into the box, and reached for her drill.

"Back to work; we're not done yet. It's six o'clock and I've got to go in two hours."

Dorothea held her side, breathing heavily.

"Christine, just do as I said and have a quick clean-up here—then it'll all be good."

Laughing softly, she followed Ines and helped to hold the curtain rails while she fixed them in place.

We'd met that morning at my new apartment. My furniture and moving boxes had arrived the day before. Along with Ines, I'd helped with the unloading, lugged everything inside, and then had promptly burst into floods of tears. So Ines had decided that the unpacking, drilling, and screwing could wait until the next morning. Dorothea, who had jumped to offer her help, arrived in the best of moods and could hardly wait to get going. Ines brought her toolbox and oversaw the proceedings, gave directions, crossed things off her list, and screwed and drilled with dedication and no signs of tiring. By midday the kitchen, office, and bedroom were almost finished.

Ines and Dorothea had built things piece by piece and screwed everything together while I unpacked box after box and arranged everything.

Georg came too, laden with trays of rolls and cakes and a crate of beer.

"I couldn't make it sooner, I'm afraid. Is there anything I can still do to help?"

We all laughed. Georg was a journalist. According to Ines, his ability to work with his hands was limited to plugging his laptop in. And sometimes he couldn't even manage that! She stared at him for a while and decided that he could cope with breaking down the empty moving boxes and bringing them up to the loft.

"I'm sure you can manage that without breaking anything or hurting yourself."

Her sarcasm was like water off a duck's back.

"Without me you'd be starving and thirsty. I'm perfectly capable of folding and carrying, and besides, you all love me really."

He stayed in spite of all the teasing, and Ines gave him job after job to do. Within half an hour he had held lamps, unpacked books, made coffee, and hugged me compassionately at least twenty times. Then he had to go. For the last two hours we worked on under Ines's command, and then we drank our last beer around the dining table. Ines stretched and looked around with satisfaction.

"You can sleep properly in your own bed, your kitchen's ready, all the lamps are up, and the bathroom's cleaned. The only thing left is the rest of your unpacking and a few odds and ends. But there's plenty of time for all that. Aren't we wonderful?"

Dorothea looked at me with her big eyes and stroked her hand over the wooden table.

"But still no tablecloth." She giggled. "My darlings, I'm so done in, I'm getting all silly again. I'd love to have another beer with you, but I have to go to bed. I've got a broadcast tomorrow morning at eight."

It was eight o'clock in the evening. We'd been at it for almost twelve hours.

"Will you be okay?" asked Dorothea.

"Of course."

I was looking forward to being alone.

"I'll do a little more unpacking and then have an early night too."

"Good."

Dorothea paused behind me.

"Remember, what you dream on the first night will come true."

She kissed the top of my head.

"And you really need to get to the salon, sweetie. Graying roots may be okay out in the sticks, but not here. I'll be back tomorrow afternoon. Have fun unpacking."

I stood up too and kissed Ines on the cheek. She looked at me with a slightly worried expression.

"It's fine, Ines. Really. And thank you."

"Till tomorrow then. Sleep well on your first night."

I closed the door behind them.

And I was in my new apartment alone for the first time.

Alone

I walked slowly through the rooms. I turned the light on in each one, left all the doors open, put a floor lamp on, placed a chair next to it, and smoothed down the bedding. Most of the furniture was new; every free minute of the last two weeks had been spent with either Dorothea or Ines in furniture warehouses and household shops, buying all the things I needed for my new life.

Georg had offered to lend me money. He earned a lot, spent very little, and always had a fair amount left over. I was touched by his offer and accepted it. It enabled me to feel I could separate from the things that reminded me of my marriage. I looked around me. There were so many things in this apartment that I wasn't used to yet. It felt strange. Unfamiliar.

I took a deep breath and decided to unpack another three boxes, then shower and open the bottle of red wine that Dorothea had brought with her.

Two hours later I was sitting in my bathrobe and with damp hair in my almost-finished dining room. No tablecloth. I thought of Dorothea and smiled. But I did have a candle, a glass full of red wine, and a new CD that Georg had given me today, *Sunset Dance & Dreams*, free from any memories of Bernd.

The new lamp cast a warm glow as I looked around the room from the table. I liked the furniture and lamps that I'd bought. It was already shaping up to be a beautiful room; I felt almost content. I'd done it.

Today was April 16. Day one after the move.

In the recent days and weeks, I'd been conjuring up this date in my mind like a magic formula. April 16. I just had to keep going until then. After that things would get better. I'd managed all of my business appointments, but it was still demanding. I had stayed with Ines for the last two weeks.

My move wasn't planned until April 15; the moving company couldn't do it sooner. The apartment was available, but it was still empty because the furniture couldn't be delivered until then. Ines arranged the delivery dates for me. By day I cleaned the new apartment and called insurance, utility, and phone companies. I spent hours sitting in the residents' registration office. My back aching, I struggled around DIY shops, crossing items off of Ines's shopping lists. In the evenings I went with my sister—and her tape measure—to furniture shops and back to the same DIY shops to exchange the things on the list I had bought wrongly. I rarely seemed to know what the correct parts were.

Dorothea had us over for dinner and, with the help of lots of wine and her enthusiasm for my apartment, managed to dissipate the dark clouds that were gathering in my mind. I had brunches with Georg, and he brought along the programs for Hamburg theatres and concert halls, marking all the events that he was free for. When I still looked sad, he tried to get tickets for the Hamburg Symphony Orchestra.

I listened to all the plans, wrote Georg's free evenings in my calendar, let Ines explain the logistics of the DIY shops to me, laughed at Dorothea's jokes, and thought constantly about April 16. I just had to keep going until then. Then this awful in-between period of homelessness and worry would be in the past.

Today was April 16. I sat in my almost-finished apartment and waited for the feeling that everything would be better from now on.

You'll be waiting a long time. It doesn't just come by itself, you know.

I heard the horrible voice in my head.

In a crisis, my sister wrote lists, while I would have a dialogue in my head between two women's voices. One was out to cause trouble, and the other to calm me down. For years the two voices had made themselves heard whenever I felt helpless and was alone.

Our mother had gone to great efforts not to mollycoddle her three children. Which meant there was a certain gruffness in the way she had brought us up. On the other hand, she was always very optimistic and could sometimes be very tender. She had a hyphenated name, which had made a great impression on me as a child. Edith-Charlotte. So when I heard the voices for the first time, I named the mean one Edith and the gentle one Charlotte.

I pulled up a chair, put my feet up, and lit a cigarette. For the first time in weeks, the voices managed to find some space in my head.

You've never lived so well. A great apartment, chic furniture, right in the center of town. Life's really starting to get exciting, said Charlotte.

Exciting. Sure. You're almost forty and starting all over again, answered Edith.

I took my glass and sat down on the new sofa. Ligne Rosé. Delightful.

Even the sofa. You've wanted one like that for years. Bernd didn't; he preferred leather because otherwise you'd see the cat hairs.

My cats. I felt a pang of longing. I hadn't seen them since I left.

Leaving.

My mind went back to that day two weeks ago. Karola's birthday.

I'd driven home in a daze. On the way, thoughts and images rushed into my head thick and fast. Antje, who would have had no way of knowing what my apartment was like. Bernd's bad mood as I went off to the party. Antje, who hadn't been in touch with me for weeks despite knowing the state I was in. Bernd saying, "It's about me, not you." Ines's suspicion: "It sounds to me like there's another woman."

It was like I'd knocked over a domino. More and more situations occurred to me that had seemed odd but I had never thought any more of. The fact that Bernd had never been able to remember my mobile number, but phoned Antje from the car when we were running late. The fact that Antje, whom I used to speak to about my marital problems on our frequent trips to the sauna, had always pushed me to separate from him.

I couldn't stop the thoughts from coming.

I drove along like I was on autopilot and only became aware of my surroundings again as I parked in the drive-way. I turned the engine off and just sat there. Bernd's car was there, so he must be too. Of course, Antje would have phoned him right away, so he would have had time to make up some new stories for me.

I started the car again, put it in reverse, turned around, and drove to Marleen's. When I parked in front of her house, she saw me through the window and was standing at the door by the time I had crossed the yard. She called out, "Perfect timing. I've just put some coffee on."

She looked at my face.

"What's happened?"

"I've just come from Karola's birthday party."

"Oh. And? How was it?"

"What do you know?"

"Why don't you come in first."

A little later, we were sitting in the kitchen. Marleen talked, and I listened, feeling colder and colder.

Marleen had seen Bernd and Antje in a pub together the week after our separation. They'd only had eyes for each other and hadn't noticed her. Marleen thought it was strange, so she drove to her ex-husband's and grilled him for information. Adrian stayed silent at first and didn't want to say anything; after all, Bernd was his best friend. Eventually though, he gave in to Marleen's persistent questioning.

Their affair had started as long as four years ago when we bought the house and started to renovate it.

At the time, I was touched by and thankful for Antje's enthusiasm to help. I had a very busy schedule with work, and she sacrificed her three-week vacation to lend a hand. At the time I just thought that was what you did when you'd been friends for twenty-five years. Each day I had gone to the bookstores while Antje and Bernd renovated and Adrian, who was there every day too, looked on.

After two weeks he took Bernd aside and had a word. Bernd seemed to show some discretion and put the whole thing on ice.

"Antje and I had a strange fight back then, come to think of it. She accused me of not having offered her anything for her help. I really didn't understand at the time."

"There's no way you could have understood. What she wanted was your husband."

Marleen took a cigarette, even though she didn't smoke.

"In any case, it didn't stay on ice for long. It seems that things kept happening between them, and last summer she went in for the kill."

"I didn't notice anything."

"Then in December she started to put pressure on him. Apparently she really flipped out when you both went to your parents' place over Christmas and then stayed there for New Year's too."

"How did Adrian know that?"

"Bernd told him everything almost as soon as it happened. She was in a foul mood all through January and threatened Bernd that if he didn't tell you about the affair, she would. Then you went to your neighbor's birthday party, and it all came to a head. You went to stay with Ines on Monday morning. Antje came to see Bernd that evening and wanted to know how you'd taken the news. That was, it seems, the deadline. That's why he phoned you."

I felt both hot and cold at the same time. I searched for words. Marleen looked at me sadly.

"I've known for six weeks. I kept going back and forth and thought that it would tear the whole world out from under your feet if you found out now. I wanted to wait until you were settled in your new apartment and wouldn't have to see either of them anymore."

"She wanted to help me with the move. Just imagine, the old Jezebel wanted to help me with the move, and…" My tears started to fall.

"She probably wanted to make sure that you didn't take everything." Marleen shook her head. "The next day, when you were back with Ines, I drove to see Bernd. I had such a go at him that he was as white as a sheet. I told him that if that backstabbing woman so much as set foot on the property before the fifteenth, I'd see to it that the whole house was completely emptied. After all, you paid for everything."

"I just can't believe it. It's like a bad movie. I look after her children, and she's out fucking my husband. Shit, twenty-five years of friendship—what kind of person is she? I could kill her, the little rat."

"Just make sure you don't leave too many things for them."

"I don't want any of it. It's all just false memories."

Marleen pressed my hand.

"I understand, but don't leave everything. Take what you want to take."

We were both exhausted and fell silent for a while.

"Marleen, I feel awful. I'm going to go and pack everything now and put yellow labels on the furniture that I want to take. Would you be able to go over on the fifteenth and make sure that everything gets brought along?"

"Of course. Shall I come and give you a hand now?"

"No, I have to do it myself. I'll write a list of which pieces of furniture and how many boxes and so on."

We finished smoking our cigarettes in silence and drank the rest of the coffee, and then I stood up. Marleen took me in her arms and pulled me close.

"In half a year's time we'll be laughing about it. Keep your head high."

Just as I was about to open the front door, it was flung open from the inside. Bernd stood in the hallway with a sheepish grin. I went silently past him. I couldn't look him in the face.

"So, how did it go with the kids?" he asked.

I swallowed, pressing my fingernails into the palms of my hand.

"I'm sure you've already been on the phone with her. I left three hours ago. What do you think?"

"Christine, you've got it all wrong. It all started after we separated; I was so lonely."

I looked at him. Until now I'd had no idea how much it could hurt to look into the face of someone you had lived with for years.

"I can't believe that you're this pathetic."

I went upstairs and started packing. It took until five the next morning. By then I'd packed up my whole life, marked the few bits of furniture that I wanted to take with yellow labels, filled up my car, and written the list for Marleen. Once I was done, I sat in the kitchen, had a cup of coffee, and smoked the last cigarette I would ever smoke in this house. My cat jumped up onto my lap, and the tears came.

You will not run out of here crying! Pull yourself together!

Thanks, Edith. At that moment Bernd came into the kitchen.

"So, all packed?"

"Marleen will come by on the fifteenth when the moving men come. I've made a list of the things that I'm taking. Most of it I'm leaving here, so don't even try to argue."

"Christine, I'm sorry."

"Save it. It makes me feel sick just thinking about it."

I pushed past him and left that house and that life.

For the first time ever, I slammed the door. Hard.

My new CD had finished. I stood up and set it to play again.

But today is April 16. You've got a new apartment, a new life, and it's all behind you now.

Thanks, Charlotte.

I looked at the new clock—12:05 a.m. Day two.

I drank the last of my glass of wine, took it through to the kitchen, and put it in my new dishwasher.

Everything will get better from here. The only way is up. You're past the worst, said Charlotte.

It won't be easy; there's a long and hard way to go yet, countered Edith.

I turned the music and the light off, went into my bedroom, and lay down on my freshly made bed. Lying there, I felt the tears begin to prick behind my eyes. I turned my thoughts to Marleen, Dorothea, and Ines and hoped for good dreams.

Misery

When I woke up the next morning, my neck and head hurt.

It was seven o'clock, and my first thought was, *We've overslept; Bernd has to leave at seven.*

The second followed swiftly behind: *I'm alone.*

I felt miserable, but I couldn't lie there anymore. My back aching, I crawled out of bed and went into the bathroom. My reflection looked just like I felt. Spotty skin, greasy hair, unplucked eyebrows, dark rings and bags under my eyes.

It's no wonder Bernd didn't want to be with you anymore. Just look at yourself.

I hated Edith's voice, but I leaned in closer to the mirror anyway. It wasn't just that my eyes were red and gunky; now they were swimming with tears. I glanced at the clock on the sink. Seven fifteen. Still so early. I was cold, and it hurt to swallow. As I bent over to pull on my tights, I started to feel dizzy. I sat down on the bathtub for a moment, and the dizziness gradually began to pass.

If you pass out now, you'll be lying here the whole day, alone.

The fit of tears came on as suddenly as the dizzy spell had. I'd never cope, I didn't have the strength for all the new beginnings, everything familiar was gone, and the next few days loomed in front of me as heavy as lead. Where would I start?

It was only when I felt my ice-cold feet that I sat up straight. I made myself breathe steadily, slowly pulled on my dressing gown and thick socks, and blew my nose.

And now go to the kitchen, make yourself a cup of coffee with your new machine, sit yourself down, and plan out your day in peace.

I made plans every morning. But every movement was labored and lethargic. I was settling in at a snail's pace, but because I had to, not because I wanted to. Whenever Ines or Dorothea came by, I pulled myself together; it was easier then.

I had to pull myself together again when Dorothea went to Finland for three weeks on a painting holiday just three days after I moved in, and when Ines said her goodbyes just one day later to go sailing for two weeks. My sister had done enough for me recently; she'd earned the vacation. But even so, I felt like I'd been thrown into the deep end. Before she left she told me to give my friends and colleagues in Hamburg a call. Hardly anyone knew that I was living there yet.

I said I would, but I didn't phone anyone. I didn't have the energy yet to talk to anyone about Bernd.

Since they'd both been away, the minutes and hours were crawling by. I got a bad cold and blamed it for the way I was feeling. Everything I did took effort. Thinking of Ines and her lists, I wrote a plan for the week.

Monday: Set up a mailbox.
Tuesday: Go to the supermarket.
Wednesday: Buy curtains for my office.
Thursday: Go to the hairdresser.
Friday: Buy flowers and window boxes.

I didn't achieve a single one of them. Everything was too much effort. I had to force myself just to shower and wash my hair each day. I hadn't put makeup on in days. At six o'clock I put the television on and drank red wine, drank until the bottle was empty and I fell asleep in the chair. Somehow I still managed to brush my teeth and stumble to bed. Then I had a dream about Antje and Bernd and woke up at seven the next morning with my eyes puffy and red from crying.

This was how the first few weeks of my new life went—gray, miserable, and immeasurable.

On Friday evening Marleen phoned again. She was the first person I'd spoken to that day, and my voice was throaty and hoarse from smoking. I was also tipsy. The conversation lasted ten minutes and ended with her telling me she'd be getting on the twelve thirty train to see me the next day. Suddenly sobering up, I looked around my new apartment. I hadn't done anything for days, there were clothes lying everywhere, unpacked boxes were still all over the hallway, and neither the bathroom nor the kitchen were clean.

I made myself a cup of coffee and got down to work.

I was on the platform before the train arrived. I'd showered, epilated my legs, plucked my eyebrows, blow-dried my hair, and put makeup on. Pulling on my best pair of jeans, I'd realized that they were at least a size too big for me. I thought of Antje's constant diets and felt Charlotte smile. I saw Marleen right away. She was hauling three big bags filled with plants and a travel bag. Once she stood in front of me, she looked me up and down sternly.

"You're all thin and you look like crap. I can see we've got a lot of work to do."

Then she gave me a big hug.

"First I want to see the finished apartment and dump these plants. They're all offshoots; I bet you haven't planted the balcony or the terrace yet. After that we'll go shopping. Judging by how you look, I can well imagine what you don't have in your fridge at the moment. Besides that I want to go clothes shopping, and only the best places, mind; I've got money burning a hole in my pocket."

Once we got to my apartment she was enthusiastic, not commenting on the fridge or the empty bottles stacked in the box under the kitchen counter.

An hour later we drove into the parking lot in front of the supermarket. I had tried to go shopping here just once. My cart had already been half full when I got to the pet food aisle. I froze and thought, *You'll never buy cat food again.* I looked at the contents of my cart. There was too much; I'd been buying for two people out of habit. As the tears came, I left the cart there and fled to my car.

After that I just went to the gas station around the corner from time to time.

There was a bottle bank in front of the supermarket. Marleen opened the trunk of the car and unloaded the box with my empty spoils.

"Come on, I won't say a word, but you can at least help me get rid of them."

There was a shocking number of bottles. An older couple looked over at us. I felt caught in the act and looked at Marleen guiltily. Unmoved, she threw one bottle after the other in the bank and looked over at me.

"It must have been one great party, hey?"

I couldn't help but smile.

In the afternoon we went into town. Marleen wanted to buy lingerie, and her craving for retail therapy was infectious.

"So, Christine, now you pick out something stunning for yourself. For the future. I'd like to treat you to something."

I didn't argue.

Laden down with bags and packages, we stopped for a coffee break in Café Wien, a disused longboat on the Alster Lake. We looked out over the water, drank Prosecco, and smoked. For the first time in weeks, I felt alive again.

Marleen looked at me. "You've taken your time out and you've suffered. Okay. You needed to do it, and it was exactly the same for me after my separation from Adrian. But there has to be a point when it stops. You can't let that asshole and old cow get the better of you. I won't let you. You'll show them, you'll see."

"It's so hard though."

"Yes, it is. But you've already got past the worst of it. It's May now. Your birthday's in November, still half a year away. By then, we'll be laughing about it."

On Sunday evening I dropped Marleen off at the station. My balcony had flowerpots full of flowers. Her cuttings hadn't been enough, and she'd almost fallen over with laughter when she saw that the flowers I'd picked out at the nursery were called "Man's Loyalty."

I had curtains in my office, and my fridge and storage cupboards were full.

The evening before we had treated ourselves to a special meal in a restaurant on the harbor, topped off by four "Sex on the Beach" cocktails in a nearby bar. Afterwards, we sat up in my kitchen until the early hours, reading our horoscopes aloud from magazines she'd bought at the station. For the first time in a long while my tears were of laughter, not sadness.

I stayed on the escalator until the train disappeared from sight. Then I turned around and went back to my car.

I felt like I was going home.

Changes

The sun shone down on my face as I came back from the post office at midday. I'd finally applied for a mailbox. When I'd told Marleen that I still had to get around to it—fearing what to write next to "marital status"—she had rolled her eyes.

"Good gracious, you're renting a mailbox, not adopting a kid."

The whole thing lasted just four minutes; I shook my head at myself, but I was bursting with pride.

Standing in the entrance hall to my building, I heard my phone ringing inside the apartment. Before I could get the door open, the answering machine clicked on. As I listened, my exuberant feeling faded away.

"Hi, Christine, it's Hans-Hermann here. I ran into Bernd yesterday evening, and he told me about…well, your news. So, of course we need to have a talk. After all, you're still paying for the house and so on. Give me a call and we'll make an appointment for you to come in, preferably with Bernd there too. See you soon."

Hans-Hermann was my tax consultant.

I'd been suppressing thoughts about money and the future. I knew, of course, that we had to deal with the financial side. We were both still paying the mortgage, and on top of that I had an automatic deposit going into Bernd's private account every month. I'd started doing it while he was still studying but never stopped it; after all, we spent our money on things for both of us.

But not anymore.

I went out onto the balcony and felt the soil in the flowerpots. Marleen had done a great job. It looked like paradise. The phone rang again. This time it was Dorothea.

"Sweetheart, I've made an appointment for you with Holli—you know, my sensational hairdresser. It's this evening at six. I'll pick you up. I've told him he needs to make a country bumpkin into a glamorous diva who looks ten years younger. That sounds good to you, right? How are you today?"

"My tax consultant just called. I've got to set a meeting with him and Bernd to talk about the finances."

"Don't tell me you haven't done that yet? Are you still supporting him?"

"I hadn't gotten around to it yet."

"That's the very first thing I'd do. You must be out of your mind!"

"But I didn't want to see him."

"Of course not, you'd just prefer to keep sticking money where the sun doesn't shine while he takes that old toad out for fancy dinners."

"Dorothea!"

"It's true though. Just make the appointment as soon as you can. If Ines or Georg get wind of this, they'll kill you."

"I'll call him now."

"You'd better. I'll pick you up at five thirty then. See you later."

I kept the phone in my hand.

"Christine, what are you two playing at?" asked Hans-Hermann as soon as I'd said hello.

"I'd really rather not talk about it, but it's not *us*, just *him*."

"I figured as much. Your so-called better half wasn't exactly alone when I saw him. Some big blonde woman. She looked familiar to me somehow."

The thought cut me to the quick.

"Are you still there?"

I tried to find my voice.

"Yes. Okay, then at least you know the score. You wanted me to make an appointment with you?"

"It's you that should want to after what's happened. I'm sorry, I hope I didn't put my foot in it. Just to make things clear, you've been my client for ten years, but I'll handle the whole thing fairly. It's completely inappropriate that you're still supporting Bernd financially. What do you want to happen with the house? Do you want it back, or are you staying in Hamburg?"

"I definitely don't want to go back. I don't care what happens to it."

"I got the impression that Bernd wants to keep it. But that means he'll have to pay the mortgage by himself and pay you an indemnity. We'll have to figure out the details. Are you up to a meeting between the three of us?"

"Hans-Hermann, I'm a big girl now. I'm not the type to make a scene. And if I make a lunge for him, you can always break it up."

He didn't answer.

"That was a joke."

"Ah, okay. Will you call him or shall I?"

"I'd appreciate it if you could."

He wrote down a few possible dates, and then we said goodbye.

I sat out on the balcony and lit up a cigarette. My hands were shaking.

"Your so-called better half wasn't alone."

They certainly weren't wasting any time.

What did you expect? For them to have a year of mourning? They're as happy as larks, said Edith.

My newfound lightheartedness had disappeared. I felt sick, imagining Antje and Bernd walking hand in hand through our old house. Once again, the telephone rang and interrupted my thoughts.

I said hello and was instantly annoyed at how weak my voice sounded.

"Hi, it's me."

My stomach churned. Bernd.

"Hello."

Terse, but controlled.

"How are you?"

"Fine thanks. What do you want?"

"I ran into Hans-Hermann at Carlo's yesterday. We had a chat and quite a few drinks. It was a good laugh."

The thought of the three of them laughing together brought gastric acid to my throat.

"I've just been on the phone with him. We've got to make an appointment. I've told him what dates I can do, so you give him a call and work something out."

"Are you angry or something?"

I hung up. This time my tears were of rage, not sadness.

When Dorothea rang the doorbell at five p.m., my throat was still sore. But I'd managed to take a bath, put a nice outfit on, and took care doing my makeup. The façade looked okay.

In the car I told Dorothea about the phone calls, and that Hans-Hermann had called back to confirm our appointment for next Wednesday.

"So that'll be the first time you go back there. Do you want me to come with you?"

"I'll be okay by myself. But thank you."

In the meantime, Dorothea had parked her Mini up at the Gänsemarkt.

"In any case, you'll need to look fantastic when you go."

The hairdressing salon was a proper temple of beauty—lots of chrome, lights, and leather. Holli turned out to be Hamburg's answer to Johnny Depp. A gay version.

"Dora, honey! How lovely! And you look fabulous! How's your life and love life? Glass of champers?"

Without waiting for an answer, he whirled through the salon and came back with two glasses.

"So ladies, welcome, welcome."

He took a close look at me, then looked at Dorothea.

"So, what's the artist's brief?"

I had to suppress my laughter; it was like being in a movie.

"Holli, this is Christine. She's just separated from her husband and is finally in the big city. She just doesn't look the part yet."

"Well, I can see that."

He eyed me critically, ran his fingers through my hair, and brushed it from my face.

"This bob is boring, frightfully boring. It's got no dynamic, no pep, and then these grays. No, honey, this just won't do. We'll do something completely different."

Dorothea settled into a chair with some glossy magazines and champagne while I took my place on the scarlet hairdresser's chair. I shut my eyes while Holli gently washed my hair. During the head massage that followed, he looked me straight in the eyes in the mirror.

"I always say, 'A new life needs a new hairdo.' We'll make you into a completely new woman. Smart and bouncy, not so dowdy. This is a new start."

"I'm not sure—that sounds so different…"

"Sweetheart, this is my job. Okay?"

Two hours later Dorothea and Holli stood behind my chair, hardly able to contain their enthusiasm. I looked in the mirror. My hair was now shorter and fell loose and wild. It was a shiny chestnut brown. I looked completely different. Holli's beautiful colleague Tabea had given me a professional makeover. She'd introduced herself as a stylist. I wondered whether having a name like Tabea was a prerequisite for a job like this. You probably wouldn't get far if you were called Doris.

My eyes looked very big. And very blue.

"Look at her, Dora—ten years younger and so striking, but kind of hip too."

The bill was pretty hip as well. I didn't bat an eyelid, but it was a struggle. I'd never spent so much money at a hairdressing salon in all my life. But then, my old hairdresser *was* called Doris.

Outside, Dorothea grasped my shoulders.

"You look amazing. We have to celebrate. We'll go have dinner and then hit the town."

I was already feeling the effects of the champagne, and my soul felt as light as my new hair.

We ate at Wide World, one of my favorite restaurants. Dorothea told me stories of the TV world, each one funnier than the last. I worried about my expensive eye makeup running. Later, two of her colleagues joined our table. Marcus and Peter were makeup artists, good friends of Holli, the "artist," and they called me "sweetheart" too. They'd come into the bar by chance, recognized Dorothea's gleeful squeals of laughter, and came over to us.

They were charming and great fun. We talked and laughed and ordered one bottle of wine after the other. Listening eagerly to Dorothea, they were touched by her indiscreet stories about my metamorphosis from country duckling into city swan, and they burst into horrified laughter throughout. Once they'd heard everything, Marcus took my hands in his in a dramatic gesture.

"Oh sweetheart, what an idiot that man was. Just be happy that it's over. How awful!"

I was moved, feeling tipsy and at ease in their company.

Peter raised his glass. "So, let's call an end to the sad stories. Summer's starting, and we're going dancing."

I hadn't danced in what seemed liked forever. It was mid-week and already midnight. It felt daring. I felt a boundless lust for life surge within me. We danced and drank until four the next morning. It was intoxicating; I didn't think, I just listened to the music and looked into the laughing faces of Dorothea, Marcus, and Peter.

Sitting in the cab later, I felt exhilarated. I hoped the cab driver would be able to figure out the address I'd given him. My articulation hadn't exactly been clear. He asked me again, but my second attempt wasn't much better. In any case, he drove off. The journey through Hamburg at night was wonderful, but the cab stopped after just a short drive. I recognized my house and was relieved. The display on the meter was blurry, so I pressed a note into his hand without having really understood the price. It must have been too much though, because he opened the door for me and shook my hand goodbye. In my very tipsy state, I found him very charming, and I stayed on the pavement to wave him goodbye. Once the brake lights had disappeared, I made my way hand over hand along the box tree hedge to the front door. Suddenly, I lost my balance and fell, landing in the hedge, which opened up, closed around me, and then slowly let me slip down onto the lawn.

I lay there like an upturned beetle on my back, eyes shut, and tried to figure out if anything hurt. Nothing did. Then I opened my eyes. The stars were twinkling above me.

I lay there, with my hip hairdo and my beautiful eyes. I looked up at the sky and burst into laughter.

Putting Things in Order

surveyed myself critically in the mirror.

Dorothea tugged at the collar of my blazer. She flicked a hair from my shoulder, looking content with what she saw.

"Perfect," she said, looking me over from head to toe.

I was skeptical. "Isn't it a bit too much?"

"Nonsense, you want that idiot to see what he's given up. I think you look great."

"Dorothea, I look like some TV Barbie doll."

"Of course you do—the clothes are from the wardrobe at work. And, by the way, TV Barbies are all I know." She laughed.

I was wearing a brown pinstripe suit with narrow trousers and a long jacket. With a skintight white T-shirt with a deep neck. My lingerie was invisible, and I could barely feel it. A thong, so there would be no VPL under the slim-fitting trousers, and a Wonderbra to give me cleavage. Both scarlet red.

"It's an old TV trick," Dorothea had explained as she took the mere hints of lingerie from the bag. "You can't see red under white." I was impressed. Dorothea knew her stuff, and she'd made me into someone completely different. I was almost the city swan. The only thing missing was the blasé facial expression. I puckered my lips, which were painted dark red, and blew her a kiss in the mirror.

"I've never dressed up like this to go to the taxman before."

"It's not Hans-Hermann you want to make an impression on. I'd love to see Bernd's face when he sees you looking like this."

She rubbed hair wax on the tips of her fingers and gave my hairdo one last polish. Then she looked at my cleavage.

"Didn't your ex-best friend Antje always wear those sports bras? You know, those white cotton things that showed off her droopy boobs so well?"

"Dorothea! Why are you bringing that up now?"

"I'm just saying. If you feel a bit meek at any point, just think of the knock-out lingerie you're wearing. That'll make you feel superior again, no problem."

I couldn't help but laugh. Antje did wear those sports bras.

After one final look in the mirror, and one that made me feel satisfied, I picked up my bag and car keys. We left my apartment together. Dorothea waved as I set off to see Hans-Hermann, driving the old route for the first time since the move.

As I drove over the Elbe Bridge, I started to feel a bit flat. I hated confrontations about money, found tax explanations and the subject of separate bank accounts very unpleasant, and on top of all that, I'd be seeing Bernd again for the first time in weeks. The night before Georg had impressed on me the importance of listening to Hans-Hermann's advice and of speaking up for myself.

"Bernd wants the house without you in it, so he has to make do without your money as well. Don't let yourself be talked into paying for something just because you don't like confrontation."

Georg had looked at me insistently.

"You financed his studies and paid for most of that house. The least he can do now is offer to pay for the things you left there."

"But he never has any money."

"Christine, that's not your problem. Please stay firm for once."

I had promised to at least try. What would Bernd look like? And what would he think about how different I looked? I turned the rearview mirror towards me. Slim face, shiny hair, big eyes. Tabea and Dorothea had shown me all the tricks.

Charlotte piped up.

You've never looked so good. And those clothes! Just imagine the look on his face. And that's even without seeing your lingerie.

Edith's response was close behind.

As if that would matter to him. Besides, he prefers big blondes. With droopy boobs, added Charlotte.

By now I was almost there.

It was a strange feeling. I knew every street here, every house, had driven down these roads countless times. It was all familiar, but in spite of that I didn't belong here anymore. It hurt.

Charlotte tried to salvage things.

What do you want out here in the sticks anyway? It smells of manure and silage, and there are old run-down farms everywhere.

Think of your apartment, the Alster Lake, the city, the bright lights, the people.

I took a deep breath as I drove into the parking lot at the tax office. I couldn't see Bernd's car, but maybe it was still too early. My pulse quickened; in less than half an hour I would have to see him. Hans-Hermann opened the door to me and smiled in disbelief.

"Wow, is that what people look like in Hamburg when they're getting a divorce? Christine, you should have done it sooner. Sorry, I mean, even before you looked…I mean, don't get me wrong, but now…I mean, wow."

I shook his hand.

"Don't worry, I know what you mean. Thank you."

"Come on in then; we can make a start right away. I've already got all the files out and worked out a few suggestions. I've asked Bernd to come half an hour later. He's evidently not so keen on you pulling your money out, but he'll have to bite the bullet."

We sat down in his office, and Hans-Hermann explained his recommendations to me while I tried to pay attention. With the help of columns of figures and bank statements, he divided up my twelve years of marriage with Bernd. I forced myself to concentrate and keep my composure, to remember it's just about money, not feelings, just money.

I made a big effort to concentrate and became so wrapped up in the task at hand that I only looked up when Hans-Hermann's secretary opened the door. Suddenly, Bernd was standing in front of me. My heart stopped.

Awkwardly, he shook Hans-Hermann's hand first, then mine. He avoided my gaze, sat down on the edge of the third seat, and said, "Well, have you already made a deal?"

Stunned, I tried to catch my breath. Not a word to me, no greeting, instead he was just acting as if I were trying to cheat him out of something. A wave of rage surged within me. Hans-Hermann touched my arm fleetingly and gave me a warning look. Then he turned to Bernd, smiling.

"My dear man, we aren't 'dealing' here at all. As you know, I manage your soon-to-be ex-wife's accounts, and there are future details connected to that which do not concern you. But we're done with her things now and can look at the joint funds together." He began to explain how we should go about separating our marriage financially.

I was trying so hard not to look at Bernd that it wasn't long before I lost track of the conversation. Bernd asked questions, and Hans-Hermann answered. I didn't say a word and left everything to him. I couldn't understand any of it, and my mind was full of thoughts of lingerie and sports bras.

"Christine, are you in agreement with that?"

Startled, I looked at Hans-Hermann, who had asked the question.

Bernd was watching me impatiently.

"I can't afford any more than that," he said.

I hadn't even been listening, and I had no idea how much or what for. Hans-Hermann started summarizing everything, so I forced myself to pay attention. Bernd had to pay me fifteen thousand euros, the sum that Hans-Hermann had calculated as an indemnity. To do that Bernd would be taking out a loan, in addition to our former joint one which he would now be taking over. The rest would be decided at the divorce.

Bernd didn't look at me once through the entire discussion. I stared at his knees, his profile, and was overcome by the urge to shake him and scream at him. Everything about him seemed so familiar. I had bought his shirt, I had ironed his jeans, I had caressed his face, I had slept beside him. And yet he wouldn't even look at me.

Within two hours everything had been sorted out. At least, that was the impression Hans-Hermann gave. He stood up, shook our hands, and gave me a wink.

Bernd followed me out to the parking lot. As we got down there, I stopped and turned to face him. He stepped to the side and walked past me, touched my shoulder lightly, and said, "Okay then, let's talk on the phone sometime. Have a good day."

"You can't just leave me standing here like this."

"Christine, come on, we've already discussed everything, and I'm not in the mood to talk anymore. Have a good day."

I bit down on my lower lip to suppress the rage and despair that were threatening to force their way out as tears. Shaking, I watched as he got into his car and drove away.

Sex on the Beach

sat in the car and smoked two cigarettes back to back. Only then did the shaking start to fade. My emotions were all over the place. I was angry, I felt humiliated, then sad again. I wanted to scream at Bernd and kiss him—all at the same time. He hadn't made even the smallest effort to be friendly, no word about how he was, no question about how I was doing. He hadn't even looked at me. I had made such an effort, and for this. The thought of my red lingerie brought tears to my eyes.

Charlotte's voice was strict.

You're wearing that for you, just like the rest of the clothes. It's your new life, the new Christine. Bernd doesn't play a part in it anymore. It's up to him to figure out how he should deal with everything. You're shaking him off, along with your old life. Don't let him give you the cold shoulder. Just wait—you'll show him, and everyone else.

Edith answered.

But he's probably driving straight to Antje's now to go to bed with her. She doesn't need a fancy thong.

My despair won out over my rage. I sat in my car, unable to think clearly, with no idea where I wanted to go. Charlotte helped.

You could go home, to Hamburg, go out for a meal with Dorothea or Ines, or to Marleen's, or wherever you want. You're free to do whatever you want, you look great, the weather's lovely, and you've got money, so just go.

At that moment my cell rang. I fished it out of my bag, looking at the number on the display. My mother. I counted to three out loud to drive the tears from my voice, and then I picked up the call.

"So, my darling, where are you?"

"I'm in the parking lot at my tax consultant's office. We just finished."

"Oh yes, that was today. How did it go?"

"To be honest, I'm not really sure. I've got all the paperwork with me, so I'll have to take a proper look through it later."

"And how was Bernd?"

"Strange."

"Strange how?"

"Oh, Mom, I can't explain that over the phone. Just strange."

"Well, come here then. If you set off now, you'll be here in time for coffee. I still have some cheesecake left. There are some of your clothes upstairs, the weather's beautiful, and you could even go to dinner with Jens this evening."

"What? Jens is there?"

"Yes, since Friday. Hanna and Klaus are getting a new heating system installed, and he's helping them with it. I ran into him this morning at the bakery and told him everything."

"You told him everything about what?"

"About how Bernd mutated into an asshole and that you've separated from him."

"Mom!"

"I phrased it more nicely. Well, not that nicely, to be honest. Anyway, he wanted to give you a call. He'll be happy to see you, and it'd do him good to get away from his parents' place for an evening. Are you dressed nicely? He looked really good."

I thought briefly of my red lingerie and turned the key in the ignition.

Three hours later I was driving over the Hindenburg Dam. The water on either side of the motorail was glistening, the sun was shining through my sunroof, and I felt happy with my decision to go to Sylt rather than back to Hamburg.

And then there was Jens.

I'd known him my whole life. His family had spent their holidays at our next-door neighbor Erna's each year. Jens and his sister Maike had been a familiar part of our summers, along with their parents Hanna and Klaus. Ten years ago Erna had decided to sell her house and move to Denmark to be near her son. She offered it to Hanna and Klaus, who were retiring that same year. They jumped at the chance and had been our neighbors ever since, which had made us all happy and the absence of Erna easier to bear.

Jens and Maike still lived in Berlin. Jens worked in a bank, and Maike was a doctor. Both had families, and we saw each other only now and then, but we were always kept up to date on each other by our parents. I tried to remember when I'd last seen Jens. He'd celebrated his fortieth

two years ago and had invited Bernd and I. We couldn't
go; I was at the book fair, and Bernd, typically, didn't want
to go to Berlin just for the day. So I'd just spoken to Jens
on the phone.

It was the summer before last that I'd last seen him.
Klaus was celebrating his sixty-fifth birthday, and everyone was there. It was a great party, apart from the fact
that Bernd was already so drunk by ten o'clock that he
had to go to bed, and Jens's wife Silke, also drunk, had
tried to hit on my brother. When Georg politely refused
her advances she had started to swear, so Jens drove her
home, returning an hour later embarrassed and full of
apologies.

"You know, she doesn't normally drink, so she can't
handle it."

Georg shrugged his shoulders and smiled. Ines looked
at Jens and then whispered to me, "Why did a nice guy like
him marry such a dumb twit?"

I shook my head and went over to Jens. "Come on, let's
have a dance; don't get worked up. Bernd's tendency to
drink himself into a coma isn't that amusing either."

We partied until four in the morning and had a great
time. I hadn't seen him since that night.

When I arrived at my parents', my mother was standing
in the front yard chatting with Hanna. They both came
towards me as I got out of the car. My mother was the first
to reach me, giving me a big hug.

"You're here in good time! The coffee's ready, and your
dad's in the yard."

I switched into Hanna's arms.

"Child, you've gotten all thin! Jens will have to feed you up properly tonight. I've already told him that you're coming. He's at the DIY shop with Klaus, but that won't take long. I told him to pick you up afterwards."

With some effort, I freed myself from her grasp and caught my breath.

"Thank you, Hanna. Just tell him to come whenever's best for him; I'll be ready."

Hanna gave us a little wave and stepped over the low fence back into her yard. Over coffee I told my parents about the financial settlement, how the appointment had gone, about the new things I'd bought for my apartment, and about my new life in Hamburg. They were relieved that everything was going well, without them having to worry too much about me.

"You'll figure everything out," said my father. "Admittedly, I never thought that Bernd would turn out this way, but that can't be helped. Just imagine, he lets you pay for his studies and the house, and then as soon as that's all done, he looks for another woman. And one with two children to boot."

My mother nodded. "I feel sorry for the children. What have they said about it?"

"I haven't seen or spoken to them since Karola's birthday. They haven't been in touch."

My father shook his head. "It's disgusting. They've probably told them something ridiculous. No, no, I hate hearing about stories like this."

My mother looked at me. "Are you staying as you are or changing? What you've got on looks great, so stay like that. I'm sure Jens will be here soon. Just brush your hair and put some perfume on."

I finished my coffee and stood up.

"I'll do it now; I'm just going upstairs."

Standing in the bathroom and putting my lipstick on, I heard the garden gate bang, then the voices of Jens and my parents. I couldn't help but smile, and I quickly wiped the traces of lipstick from my teeth.

Whenever I thought about Jens I always pictured him as an eight-year-old boy in his little blue and white striped swimming trunks. Blond and tanned.

Edith piped up.

It's a shame you can't fall in love with someone like that, just because his eight-year-old face always gets in the way.

But it'll be a comfortable, nice evening. No complications or sensitivities, answered Charlotte.

I gave myself a nod in the mirror and went out to the yard.

Jens was sat on the deck chairs with my parents. Seeing me walk over, he stood up and came towards me. He looked good. Tall, slim, short hair, which was now more gray than it was blond. He smiled at me, bent down, and kissed me on both cheeks.

"It's about time we saw each other again. You look amazing, Christine. Short hair suits you, and that lipstick looks really good on you too."

I held him close to me for a moment. "It's great to see you, and you're right, it is about time! Shall we go? Where *are* we going, by the way?"

Jens fished his car keys out of his jeans pocket.

"I've booked a table at Osteria in Westerland; it's still the best Italian in the area."

He turned around and called out to my parents, "Now, I may get her sloshed, but I'll be sure to bring her home safely! You can trust me."

"We do, we do."

My father stood up and picked up a watering can. "Make sure you behave; don't be noisy or make a mess."

"We'll do our best."

I blew them a kiss.

"See you later."

On the journey Jens told me about his week, which he'd spent renovating the boiler room with his father after the installation of the new heating system. While they were at it, they'd renovated the basement as well. The stories he told about his father, who always knew best but still did everything wrong, were so loving and funny that he soon had me crying with laughter.

"In any case, he looked around him earlier and said that we'd done a great job. He reckoned people would notice that he'd trained as a handyman when he was a young man. Christine, my father worked in a garden center for two weeks while he was studying, and after that it burned down."

We parked up in front of the restaurant. Jens looked at me from the side and then quickly pulled the sun visor on my side down. He gestured with his head, first at my face, then at the mirror.

"Somehow your makeup was a little more in place in my memory."

I looked at my eyes: my mascara had run, giving me black smears around them.

"Oh!" I started laughing again. "Tabea the stylist didn't say anything about this."

I tried to salvage my eye makeup. Jens got out, went around the car, and opened the door for me with an exaggeratedly gallant flourish.

"Come on, Mrs. Panda Bear, we'll tuck into a few eucalyptus shoots and wash them down with a bottle of red wine."

At the entrance we were met by the buzz of voices and the scent of garlic and cheese. A cheerful waiter led us to a table in the winter garden, where the background noise and temperature were at just the right level.

As we drank Prosecco and looked at the menus, we talked about our parents and Maike, Georg, and Ines. I felt myself relaxing in the atmosphere of the garden with its view of the sea, and in Jens's company. I had almost forgotten that just a few hours ago I was going over the ruins of my marriage with Bernd and Hans-Hermann.

As if reading my thoughts, Jens looked at me questioningly. "Your mother told me earlier that you were sorting out the finances today. Did everything go okay?"

"I hope so. To be honest, I didn't really concentrate during the discussion. I hate that kind of thing anyway, and on top of that, seeing Bernd..."

I briefly told him what had been discussed and the outcome. Jens listened attentively, made comments, and offered explanations from his own experience as a banker. By the time the first carafe of red wine came, along with our starters, I'd given him the short version of the events of the last months.

He looked at me compassionately. "How are you doing?"

I thought for a moment before answering.

"I don't know. Sometimes I think it's all fine. An apartment in Hamburg, great people around me, and summer's just starting. Then half an hour later I'll be sitting alone on the balcony crying my eyes out. I can't even think about Bernd and Antje; it tears me up inside. I'm homesick for my old familiar life. In three weeks' time my work schedule will kick off again, but until then it's difficult to get into a routine. I have way too much time to think."

Jens touched my hand for a moment.

"You've already accomplished so much. Enjoy these three weeks and use them to settle in to your new life. Give yourself time. Other people take years to get back on their feet after a separation like this; you've managed it in three months."

"That's what I keep telling myself. But it still hurts."

"I don't know Bernd particularly well—after all, he only came with you a few times in recent years when we all met up—but somehow I never had the feeling that your relationship was a great love story. And I never thought he was a good match for you."

I looked at Jens and thought about what he'd just said. It was strange. Bernd and I had spent twelve years together. No one had ever asked me if ours was a great love story. No one had criticized him. But now everybody was claiming they had known all along.

Before I could answer, the food arrived—along with the second carafe of wine.

Jens raised his glass.

"Here's to you. I'm confident that everything's going to get better for you now. Cheers, Christine, and by the way—you've never looked better."

There was something in his look that confused me.

"Thanks, Jens. And now I'd like to talk about something else. How are things with you?"

He drank and put his glass down. "What is there to say? Everything's going according to plan. The children are fine, steadily and bearably reaching puberty, my job's okay, and with Silke…well, it's the same as usual. She's not the easiest person, but I've learned to live with that."

"What does that mean?"

"Our relationship is often very taxing, but then it'll get better again for a while. It depends on what mood her ladyship is in. At the moment it's one of the demanding phases, so to be honest I was very happy to get away for a week. Tomorrow evening I'll get back, we'll have an argument, and then we'll act as if everything's fine again. As usual."

"How do you mean?"

"Oh, the daily marital madness. Take this for an example: In December Silke wanted to go skiing, somewhere in Switzerland that our friends were going to. I've worked in a bank for the last fifteen years. None of the department managers can take time off in December because of the end-of-year reports. She should have known that after all these years. But no, she goes ahead and books it anyway. Without cancellation insurance. So I suggested she take a friend instead. She did, but came back in a dreadful mood, saying it was an awful trip. Two weeks later our friends showed me the photos. In the middle of most of them is my lovely wife—looking like she's having the time of her life on the slopes and in the bars. So I end up getting the cold shoulder from her until January because I apparently never show consideration for her. It's the same with everyday things too; either I do things her way or she puts me in the doghouse."

"That sounds awful."

"I try not to think about it. I don't really want to talk too much about it either. I'll get through it, and that's all there is to say. Perhaps I'll get lucky and Silke will fall in love with someone else. With someone who can offer her the world and wants her all to himself." Then he gave a little smile, saying, "If she does, I'll drive her to him."

"Jens, how long has it been like this?"

"Oh, for ages now. But that's enough of the relationship talk. We can only talk about boiler rooms, gay hairdressers, and panda bears from now on. I'll leave my car here, and we can drink ourselves silly and then walk along the beach to get a taxi from Westerland. Sound good?"

There was something endearing about him. And he was funny. Being with him was doing me good.

We managed to change the subject. We had more than enough to talk about from our childhood memories of summers together. We told each other silly stories and laughed so hard that Jens got the hiccups. I remembered how clumsy his sister Maike used to be as a child. "Do you remember the debacle with the bunk bed?"

Jens thought for a moment and then started to laugh.

"Do you mean the argument between Ines and Maike about who would get the top bunk?"

"Your mother Hanna started it. Ines got the bunk bed for her tenth birthday and wanted Maike to come over for a sleepover. She was generous and offered Maike the top bunk because she was the guest."

Jens had forgotten and asked, "Then what happened?"

"Then Hanna intervened. Maike was always injuring herself in her clumsy way, falling out of the sandbox, coming off her bike, ramming the spade into her foot at the beach—there was always some mishap. My mother and Hanna spent the whole evening demonstrating with puppets and teddy bears how easy it is to fall out of a bunk bed. First Maike started crying, then Ines, then both of them together, and Maike ended up sleeping on the bottom bunk after all. With a mattress in front of the bed, just in case Ines fell out because of being in such a state."

"Yes, that's right, but then something happened anyway, didn't it?"

"Maike fell from the bottom bunk and broke her collarbone."

Jens laughed loudly.

"Even with the mattress there?"

"Well, she landed next to it."

As the evening drew on, we told more and more stories. And drank more and more wine.

I felt warm. I'd never noticed before that he had such blue eyes. And such lovely hands.

Edith's voice came promptly.

Well, you've never stared at him like this before. Think about his little blue and white striped swimming trunks!

Charlotte answered.

He's a nice guy. He's interested. He's leaving tomorrow. And you have a good time with him.

I listened to both of them, all the while looking at Jens's hands. I hadn't had sex for eight months. And I was wearing sexy red lingerie.

"Christine, hello, you still there?"

Caught daydreaming, I looked up. His eyes were very blue. When he smiled, he had a dimple on the left-hand side. I felt drunk.

"Sorry, I was lost in thought. What did you say?"

His lovely hand was on mine. "You're sweet when you're lost in thought."

I had butterflies in my stomach.

"I said, I'll get the bill and then we can go down to the beach. Then we can…we'll see."

My heart fluttered.

Edith's voice said, *Are you crazy? This is Jens!*

Charlotte replied, *It'll be nice.*

I shook both of them out of my head and looked at Jens. My hand turned over of its own accord, my thumb and his little finger clasped together.

"Good idea."

He smiled, stroking his thumb slowly over my hand. He stared at me, holding my gaze for ages. Suddenly, the waiter appeared next to us. Without letting go of my hand for a second, Jens pulled his wallet out of his jeans, managing to pay and put the change back with just one hand.

We stood up to leave. I felt like I was being moved by some strong force as we headed for the exit. I could feel Jens walking behind me. At a narrow point in the passageway we had to stop for a moment, and I felt his hand brush over my hip. My skin tingled.

Without speaking we walked across the parking lot and towards the beach. As the last beach walkers were coming towards us, we had to walk single file along the wooden walkway that led over the dunes. Jens's hand sought mine from behind, and our fingers entangled.

Then we were down on the beach, with the sea before us and stars up above. It was still warm. Jens held my hand tightly as we walked down silently to the water's edge.

Edith: *This is such a cliché.*

Charlotte: *Stop walking.*

I stopped and looked at Jens. He clasped my neck and pulled me towards him. The first kiss was cautious. He stopped and looked into my eyes. The second kiss was urgent.

I wanted him, and I wanted him here and now. I felt dizzy as his hands pushed under my jacket, then under my top.

His warm, lovely hands.

I touched his bare skin beneath his shirt. Even more warm. He was breathing quicker, and he kept kissing me.

Edith: *What are you doing? You've lost your mind.*

Be quiet, I replied.

I pushed my hands into his jeans pockets, pulled him closer into me, felt how hard he was, heard the rawness in his voice.

"Christine, I want you."

Instead of answering, I kissed him. I couldn't stop stroking the warmth of his skin.

Entangled, we went over to one of the beach chairs. Without letting go of each other for a moment, we sank down into it, opening zippers and buttons as we went.

I still felt drunk. And more turned on than I had been in months.

My eyes were closed. I could feel his hands, his tongue. I heard the waves crash nearby, his soft groaning. As he pushed himself inside me, the hard edges of the beach chair cut into my elbows. With every thrust my skin chafed against it. The same happened to my knee. It was uncomfortable.

I opened my eyes.

Jens's face was above me, his eyes closed, his mouth slightly open.

I felt dizzy. It was good to feel him, but in spite of that something was wrong.

My knee and elbows hurt, I was in an uncomfortable position, and my mind was suddenly filled with images of children playing on the beach.

Jens groaned loudly.

His face lay against my neck. He was breathing heavily. Bernd's face came into my mind, but I shook it away. Why could I feel tears coming?

I looked at Jens and felt tenderness towards him. He was so familiar. Had been my whole life.

He lifted his head and looked at me.

Please don't say the wrong thing, I thought.

"It always looks so much easier in the films. Can you still move?" he asked.

Thank you. I had to laugh. "My knee hurts like hell."

Jens laughed too and pulled himself up.

"I think we're too old for acrobatics."

He found his jeans crumpled up in the sand and pulled them on. Then he turned to me.

"You're a wonderful woman. Thank you for this evening and for…this feeling."

He helped me get my things on, got fully dressed, and then sat back down and put his arm around me. We sat there together on the beach chair for almost an hour, looking at the sea, lost in our thoughts. I felt understood.

When we arrived back at our parents' houses, we stood in the front yard for a moment. Jens swept a strand of my hair from my face and looked at me earnestly.

"Christine…"

I put my finger to his lips.

"Sshh. It was a wonderful evening, and I had a great time. And so did you. I felt good again for the first time in ages, and I have you to thank for that. I won't regret anything tomorrow."

Jens smiled and kissed me softly on the cheek.

"Thank you. I know that you'll achieve everything you've set out to do. I'll keep my fingers crossed for you. The next man in your life is going to be very lucky."

We waved goodbye as we shut the front doors.

Lying in bed, I still had that tender feeling for him. The whole evening played out before my eyes like a movie. Hands and kisses on my skin. Gazes that really *saw* me. Then, suddenly, something occurred to me that made me feel even better: Bernd was no longer the last man I'd slept with.

There were no more traces of him on my body.

Content, I fell fast asleep.

Women and Friends

The next few days were sunny, warm, and easy, just like my feelings. I hadn't seen Jens again; he'd driven back to Berlin the very next day. There had been no calls and no texts, just as I'd assumed, and hoped.

I thought back over the evening with affection, the evening that would never be repeated. Jens had uncovered something in me that had been buried for months. But it wasn't about him or me; it was just the mood, something that neither of us had experienced for a long time.

I wanted to experience it again. It didn't matter who with.

Dark red scabs had formed on my elbows. Two days later, my mother noticed and grasped my arm tightly. "How did you do that? You used to get those from rollerblading."

I looked at the grazes and saw us both lying in the beach chair again.

"I knocked into something in the pub."

My mother looked at me skeptically.

"What's so funny? And it looks like you scraped them rather than..."

"What? Did I laugh?"

"Yes, I think…"

My cell rang at just the right moment, saving me. "Sorry, Mom, it's Leonie."

"Hi, Christine, you sound very chirpy! Are you in Sylt? I've already tried to call you at home, but figured you'd probably driven up there to make the most of the good weather."

I filled her in on the events of the last few days, although admittedly ending the story of my evening with Jens with him paying the bill.

Leonie had good instincts.

"Would he be someone for you? I saw some film years ago where the woman, who had just been left by her husband, put a note on her fridge with the numbers one to twelve on it. For every number she had to find herself a lover, and by the time twelve names were on it she would be over her heartbreak. I found it really enlightening."

Me too, I thought, thinking of my first number.

"Leonie, do you want me to make a list? Is that why you're calling?"

She laughed.

"No, it just occurred to me, that's all. I just wanted to remind you that we've got our gathering tomorrow evening. Judith has booked a table at the Italian place for eight. I can pick you up half an hour beforehand. You are still coming, aren't you?"

"I completely forgot about it. You're right, it's tomorrow. I'll leave here in the morning then. It would be great if you could pick me up."

We said goodbye.

My mother laid her paper down.

"Do you have to go back?"

"Tomorrow morning. We've had this get-together with the other book trade girls for the last five years. Two weeks before we're all due to set off on the tour, we meet up in Hamburg for a meal. And it's tomorrow evening. I'd completely forgotten about it."

"How many are going?"

"Between five and ten, depending on who has time and who's up for it. I used to stay at Ines's for the night, but I've always gone along, right from the start."

"See, and now you can just go home afterwards. It's a good thing that you're living in Hamburg now, don't you think?"

"It is." I smiled at her. "It's very good indeed."

As the train took me across the Hindenburg Dam the next day, this time in the other direction, I thought about my mood on the drive up. It seemed like ages ago.

Edith said, *Don't get ahead of yourself. Just because you had sex on the beach once doesn't mean you're over it.*

Charlotte was quick to jump in.

It wasn't just sex on the beach; it was great, actually. And it was just a taste of what's to come. The years without tenderness, all those rejections and disappointments—it's all behind you now.

Yes, I thought, I'll get to work on that at least. And Jens's name was beside number one on the list.

As I turned into my street in Hamburg, I was in a good mood, and I felt like I was coming home.

That evening, I stood in front of my wardrobe and tried to decide what to wear. I pushed one hanger after another to the side, becoming more and more dissatisfied. They were all old clothes. Dorothea's suit had only been a loan, and I'd taken it to the dry cleaner's this afternoon. The only option left was the old combination of jeans with a T-shirt and black blazer, the usual rep uniform.

I held the blazer up and searched it for blemishes. Bernd had been with me when I bought it in a little boutique in Bremen. That was less than half a year ago. I'd planned to drive to the Christmas market there and buy presents for Antje's kids. Bernd had never been up for shopping trips like that, so I was really surprised when he wanted to join me. He was in a good mood, told funny stories about work, and was very attentive. At the market, we got ourselves some mulled wine and bratwurst, watched the people go by, and got excited about the snow that was starting to fall. When Bernd's ears got cold, he bought himself a felt Santa Claus hat, and he didn't take it off for the rest of the day, which really amused me. We ambled through the city center and found great presents for Antje and the kids. Then, in the evening, we went for a meal, leaving only when the parking lot was about to close.

When we were sitting back in the car Bernd discovered his phone in front of his seat, where it had fallen from his jacket pocket during the drive out. He had nine missed calls.

In a flash, his good mood disappeared. I didn't understand the reason for his bad temper and made a few jokes to try to pacify him. He mumbled something about important clients that he wouldn't be able to reach. He stopped off at the next gas station and disappeared to the toilet for ten minutes. By the time he came back he had calmed down, but he stayed subdued.

I was so naïve. Of course he'd seen who had tried to call him nine times; she'd probably given him hell when he phoned her from the restroom. In any case, it hadn't stopped her from accepting my Christmas present.

I shook the thoughts from my mind and pulled the blazer on. It didn't matter; every piece of clothing I had was from my old life anyway. I was in urgent need of a shopping trip, and ideally one with Dorothea in tow.

The doorbell rang. Leonie was early, and she came bearing flowers. I let her in.

"Who are the flowers for? Is it one of the girls' birthdays?"

"No, they're for you, Christine." She looked around my apartment. "Everything's already arranged; you must have really slogged away. It looks great!"

"So what are the flowers for? Because I let you pick me up?"

"No, just because, for your new life. For the soul and because it's summer. Just because."

She inspected me. "You've got a tan. You look much better, not like death warmed up anymore."

I laughed. She was refreshingly direct.

"Thank you. I feel better too. I'll put the flowers in water, and then we can get going."

In the car Leonie told me who was coming and what new gossip there was. Particularly about the girls who couldn't make it. Apart from Leonie, I didn't know any of them that well. I knew about their careers of course, but nothing about their private lives. I'd always been too far away, living out in the sticks. Spontaneous get-togethers with colleagues hadn't exactly been a possibility.

When we arrived at the restaurant, Maren and Franziska were already there. They usually arrived together. They'd both been in the business for a long time and had never gotten used to the lonely nights in hotels. So for years they'd been coordinating their schedules and traveling together. They were a great team whose combined power was only held back by their respective spouses. The two men couldn't stand each other. A misguided attempt for the four of them to spend the weekend together had ended in disaster. The two women had taken it in stride and confined their time together to their work schedules. Maren was big, blonde, and cheerful with a loud voice and an even louder laugh. Franziska had a sharp way about her; Leonie found her lacking in respect, cynical, and bitchy. I found her refreshing, and I envied their closeness.

We sat down and joined them. Maren looked at me. "You look different."

"I've had my hair done."

Franziska nodded in acknowledgement. "Very chic, your hairdresser must be gay."

I was amazed. "How do you know that?"

She laughed, pulled her hair up with an exaggerated gesture, and trilled, "Darling, this style looks simply divine on you!"

Maren looked from her to me and laughed. "It's true—you've got the same haircut."

Franziska leaned over to me confidingly. "You know, sweetie, that's the way they like to cut, but I tell you what, it really suits you."

"Good evening, ladies. You can hear Maren's laughter from outside, you know."

Nina had arrived, as immaculate and well-dressed as ever. Her smooth blonde hair was held back in a neat ponytail, and she was wearing a gray trouser suit with a white blouse. Her nail polish matched her lipstick, and her shoes matched her handbag.

She brushed crumbs from the seat next to Maren and sat down. With a friendly expression, she looked around at us.

"So girls, how's it going?"

"Not bad." Franziska looked at her earnestly. "But I had hoped that you'd make a bit of an effort for meeting up with us."

Nina looked shocked. "How do you mean? What…"

Maren gave Franziska a shove and suppressed her laughter. "Nina, don't listen to that tease. Her jokes get worse the longer she's at home. It's about time the tour kicked back in."

Nina had only been a rep for three years; before that she worked in a bookshop. The first time she'd joined us at one of our get-togethers she told us that she moved into repping after her divorce because she wanted a new life. She lived in Hamburg too, had a dog, and went on diving trips. That was the sum total of what I knew about her private life.

In the last few months I'd thought about her now and again. She seemed to have her life under control, and she was friendly and easygoing. I'd contemplated giving her a call and arranging to meet up with her, maybe to ask how her divorce had been. She was the only one of my colleagues who lived alone, not counting her dog of course. After I'd found her phone number, I lost my nerve. She seemed so grown-up, it would probably be impossible for her to imagine how someone could have such problems with something like applying for a mailbox.

As I looked up, I felt Nina staring at me. I returned her gaze. Before she could say anything, Anke's arrival broke the peace.

She was a hectic woman with a loud voice and rushed movements. While she was still greeting us, she took her jacket off and, without looking, tried to hang it on the coatrack, managing to knock it over in the process. Maren and Nina stood up to give her a hand. Anke apologized profusely, and then she smoothed down her very short skirt and sat down. Her sweater, with its plunging neckline, stretched tightly over her bust. Her hair fell in all directions in a scraggly fashion, held by countless colorful hair bands.

She laughed, too loudly, and looked agitatedly around the group, as if assuring herself of our attention.

"Sorry, I had to really rush. The cab didn't arrive, and then I couldn't find my shoes. I asked Werner where he'd put them, but he's not talking to me again."

Franziska leaned over to me and whispered, "Oh God, no Werner stories, please, and next time let's buy her some clothes that are two sizes bigger." I nodded.

Anke's husband Werner was twenty years older than her and the publishing manager of a large newspaper. I'd once run into them both at the book fair. Werner had treated his wife like a child, ordering her around and interrupting her, then giving her behind a benevolent pat. In return, Anke spent his money and slept with colleagues, either his or hers. She had a tendency to talk about her life and marital problems loudly and indiscreetly in public.

Now she was looking for the waitress and calling loudly for some Prosecco. Leonie looked over at me and raised her eyebrows.

Franziska took a deep breath, but before she could say a word, Eva and Judith came around the corner. Eva and her husband owned a bookshop and lived with their two children in a Hamburg suburb. Every one of us visited her on our business trips and liked her. Judith had just turned fifty, and she had been working the North German bookstores for twenty-six years. She had married a colleague, and both of them were very committed to the job. Their circle of friends consisted predominantly of publishers, authors, and press people. They spent their vacations in Tuscany, reading nonstop, drinking only Italian wine, and chain-smoking.

Breathing heavily, Eva sat down. "Judith was so punctual picking me up, but then my darling child starting acting up. She wanted Judith to read to her, and if it wasn't for that we would have got here sooner."

Judith treated Eva's children as if they were her own; she was very fond of them. Suddenly Antje's children came to my mind. I used to be very fond of them too, back then. I looked at the faces of the women around me. Apart from Leonie, none of them knew about the events of the last few months in my life. I didn't really want to tell them either.

Judith was counting heads.

"Someone's still missing, right? I made the reservation for nine people."

"And you were right to, as always." Luise sounded like a voice-over artist, but much more beautiful. Tall, graceful, black hair, classical features, always impressively dressed. She was the kind of woman who stood out for all the right reasons and was immediately the center of attention. She sat down on the empty chair next to me. Instantly, I felt fat, with bad skin and frumpy clothes.

"Hi, Christine." Her green, perfectly made-up eyes fixed on me. "New hairdo I see—got rid of your man?"

Like a shot, the conversation around us fell silent. Seven pairs of eyes stared at me.

I summoned my courage and held Luise's gaze.

"Yes."

The silence was now a shocked one. Eva, probably sensing my discomfort, tried to salvage the situation.

"Are you staying at your sister's again today? Didn't the two of you come to our shop once?"

I looked at her.

"Yes, I've only got the one sister. But I'm not staying with her; I moved to Hamburg two months ago."

Anke's voice was piercing.

"How did none of us know about this? What happened? Have you met someone new? Tell us."

She looked eager for gossip.

Franziska shot Anke a cutting look, then looked at me encouragingly. She raised her glass in my direction.

"So, welcome to the group. Now we'll be able to meet up more often!"

Right then the waiter arrived to take our orders. The sound of chatter started up again. Luise touched my arm. "I'm sorry, I didn't mean to put my foot in it. You just looked so well and relaxed. I didn't really think it would be that. Do you want to talk about it?"

"No, I'd rather not. But it's okay, you couldn't have known."

The waiter asked me what I wanted. I ordered pasta with pesto, the only thing that I could think of that quickly. I hadn't even looked at the menu yet. Nina asked me for my new address, Judith offered her help in case I still needed it in the apartment, and Eva invited me to a reading at the bookshop in two weeks' time. At the other end of the table Maren and Leonie were already on to new topics of conversation. I regaled Franziska and Luise with stories about my hunt for an apartment, Judith was in conversation with the waiter, and Nina and Eva talked about the author who was going to read.

I took my blazer off and hung it over my chair. Anke leaned over towards me.

"Christine, you've got something on your elbow. Did you hurt yourself during the move?"

I thought, *No, writing lists actually*, and tried to keep a straight face.

"Yes, something like that. It's just a graze."

The rest of the evening passed by just like the other gatherings we'd had. We talked about books, gossiped about other colleagues, compared our schedules, and rediscovered our enthusiasm for the book trade. I looked at Leonie, who was suppressing a yawn. Even Nina was carefully rubbing her eyes. She was the first to stand up.

"So, I'll be the first to make a move. I've got an early start tomorrow; we've got a telephone conference at nine a.m. We pay at the front, right? So, I hope all of you get off to a good start with your appointments, and let's stay in touch by phone. See you soon, girls."

She winked at me and put her thumb and little finger into the sign for a telephone, telling me to give her a call. I nodded in agreement. I gave Luise, who was busy suppressing another yawn, a nod too and pulled my blazer from the back of my chair. As I pulled it on, she leaned over towards me.

"Christine, would you like to go out for dinner next week? Maybe on Wednesday?"

I was confused. We'd never had much to do with one another, and I'd never seen her as being nosy either. But I still said, "Sure."

She answered quickly. "Great. Wednesday at seven p.m. in Cox on the Lange Reihe. Okay?"

She looked at me searchingly.

"It's a date."

Leonie and I went up to pay. Maren and Franziska joined us. Then we stood chatting for a few minutes in front of the restaurant.

Franziska rolled her eyes.

"Anke really gets on my nerves from time to time. One day I'll end up wringing her neck."

Leonie shrugged.

"She's not always like that. At times I feel sorry for her."

Franziska shook her head skeptically.

"Leonie, I know you're the good cop and I'm the bad cop, but if she mentions the name Werner one more time I'll scream."

Maren looked in her handbag for her car keys. Once she'd found them she turned to me.

"By the way, in case you didn't know, my husband is a lawyer. If you haven't already got something organized, I can make an appointment with him for you."

I winced. "I'm not even sure yet if and when we're actually getting a divorce. You know, all the paperwork and taxes and everything."

Leonie gave me a horrified look. "I can't be hearing right. You're not seriously telling me you want to stay married to that asshole?"

Maren discreetly moved past the question.

"Well, the offer's there if you need it. Get home safely, and I'll see you soon. Bye!"

I watched them go, and then I followed Leonie to her car. Starting the engine, she looked at me.

"I really hope that your indecisiveness about the divorce changes. You should definitely go and see a lawyer; it's not enough just to see your tax consultant. There's still the matter of alimony and inheritance entitlements, otherwise you'll have him—along with that old trout—around your neck for years."

"Leonie, can we please stop talking about it? I'll think about it. Just not this evening."

She nodded. "Okay, fine. But I'll be bringing it up again."

After a short pause she asked, "So what does Luise want from you?"

"No idea, but she wants to have dinner with me on Wednesday. In Cox. I was surprised too."

"Cox is a real hotspot, very chic, very expensive; it suits her."

I thought about Luise. I knew nothing about her.

"Do you know much about her? I can't even imagine her outside of work."

Leonie thought for a moment.

"She's very private. I've never seen her in Hamburg apart from at our gatherings. I see the others now and again for a beer or on birthdays, but she never comes out. Judith told me that she's been living in Eppendorf with her boyfriend for years, but Judith's never met him."

"I bet he's a great guy. Beautiful women tend to have beautiful men."

Leonie nodded. "I imagine her living in a huge, old building, painted white, with designer furniture, antiques, a designer Bulthaup kitchen, and a boyfriend who looks like George Clooney and is a plastic surgeon or owns a gallery."

"Leonie, watch out for those prejudices of yours."

"Well, you can find out for yourself on Wednesday. You'll see how on the ball I am. Just ask her."

"You just want me to because you're nosy."

Leonie laughed as she turned onto my street. She stopped in front of my house, leaving the motor running.

"So, sleep well, have fun, and get her to show you some pictures on Wednesday."

I got out. "Thank you for the lift. I'll call you."

I walked towards the front door, keeping a safe distance from the hedge.

Façades

Sitting on the subway, I looked at my reflection in the window of the subway car.

My hair was neither bouncy nor hip today. I hadn't managed to style it the same. My skin looked blotchy, which I hoped was just the light. My outfit wasn't bad though. Dorothea had cleaned out her wardrobe and brought two pairs of trousers and three shirts by for me. Just looking at the labels had made me feel a little faint. I had a rough idea of what Dorothea had originally paid for them.

She shrugged. "I get everything cheaper, and besides, I haven't worn these in years. They have to go. They'll suit you, so either you take them or I'll shove them in the clothing recycling bin."

I took them.

One of the trousers was brown, wide-legged, with pockets and drawstrings on the seams. They were cut on the bias, and Dorothea—the fashion expert—said they were made for me. To go with them she gave me a white linen shirt. Before leaving my apartment I had one final glance in the mirror and had thought that I was dressed perfectly, but looking at my reflection now I was unsure again. Edith knew the reason why.

You can try as hard as you like, but you'll still look like a country bumpkin next to Luise.

Charlotte was lost for words. I sighed and ran balm over my lips instead of lipstick. I had plans to meet a colleague for dinner but was acting as if I had a red carpet premiere. My insecurity annoyed me.

Luise was perfect. Women who looked like that and yet were successful and charming at the same time always seemed to polarize opinion. Whoever met Luise was either enchanted by her or intimidated. I belonged to the second group.

I'd seen her in action in a bookshop once. I arrived too early and she hadn't finished with her appointment, so while I waited I watched her. She sat, surrounded by four booksellers, in the office area. She was speaking in her pitch-perfect voice about her books, illustrating their storylines with elegant hand movements, fixating her audience with her green eyes. They hung on her every word and ordered with abandon. Once she finished, she thanked each of them with a handshake and a smile, waved to me, and glided out of the shop. Everyone watched her go.

One of the buyers turned to me and said, "What an enchanting woman."

I didn't say a word. With a glance at his watch his expression became businesslike again. "I didn't realize it was so late already; we'll have to get a move on, but never mind, you're usually quick."

It seemed Luise's spell had already faded from the working atmosphere. Next to her, everyone seemed boring and inadequate. I had no desire to feel like that. I debated whether to cancel, saying I was ill, and go back home.

The train stopped at the main station.

Charlotte convinced me.

Just think what you were like six months ago; now you're wearing designer clothes, and you're a single woman in the big city. So come on, off you go.

I stretched my back and got off. *I'll just stay for a couple of hours and not talk about anything private,* I thought, and walked towards the escalators. As I was just a few meters from Cox I heard a voice behind me.

"Christine, wait."

Unmistakable.

I stopped, turned around, and saw Luise coming towards me. She was walking quickly, with long strides and flowing arm movements. Her black dress was knee-length, and her shoes made her look even taller. Her short red jacket shone. As if she was on a catwalk, I thought, feeling short and fat.

She came to a stop in front of me, beaming.

"You're early too; I always thought I was the only one that did that. I've really been looking forward to this evening. Shall we go in?"

She opened the entrance door and walked into Cox. I followed, feeling clumsy. The waiter who met us looked just as impressive as the restaurant in his dress suit.

I heard Edith's voice: *I hope you've got enough money; otherwise, this could be very embarrassing.*

I mentally added up the contents of my purse. I had brought my credit card too, just in case. I tried to relax.

In a loud voice, Luise gave her name to confirm the reservation of the table. The impressive waiter led us over to one by the window. We sat down. I looked around, and

Luise did the same. When I recognized three TV actors at a neighboring table I glanced at her quickly, and I wanted to say something. Seemingly unimpressed, she had already immersed herself in the menu, so I controlled myself.

After a while she looked up. "Your new hairdo looks great on you, by the way, much better than before. And you should wear white more often; you're so beautifully tanned."

I was embarrassed, and I thanked her briefly. Luise beckoned to the waiter.

"Would you like an aperitif?"

I nodded. Luise ordered two Kir Royales. I felt like a celebrity.

When the drinks arrived, Luise offered me a cigarette from a silver case. She smoked the same brand as me. So, we had at least one thing in common, I thought with a smile. I took a cigarette, and she offered me a light, staring at me with her green eyes.

"So, Christine, I won't beat around the bush. I want to talk to you about your breakup."

I choked and started coughing so much that my eyes filled with tears. Luise watched me quietly, waiting until I calmed down again. I tried to catch my breath.

"Sorry, I choked."

"So I saw. All better now?"

"Yes, thanks."

I drank some water. Then I looked her straight in the eye.

"Why do you want to know about it? I never had you down as being particularly nosy."

"No, it's not about being nosy; I gave the wrong impression. It's just that…well, I've never spoken to anyone about this. I'm in a bit of a bad situation at the moment. I've been contemplating separating from my partner for months and keep losing my nerve each time I try to see it through. I'm scared. And then I saw you the other night. You looked completely different; tanned, great hairdo, and you seemed so well-adjusted and happy. Over the course of the evening it occurred to me that maybe you could help me, tell me how you managed it."

She means me, I thought, flabbergasted.

The waiter came back with his notepad poised.

"Have the ladies decided?"

"Do you eat fish?" Luise asked me.

I nodded, but stayed silent.

Luise glanced briefly at the menu. "Good, then we'd like a bottle of Sancerre and two of the fish tasting menu."

She clapped the menu shut and handed it to the water.

"Serve the wine very chilled please."

The waiter nodded assiduously and went.

I stared at Luise. Perhaps she'd just been joking.

"You look so pensive, Christine. This is my treat, by the way."

I protested. "Nonsense. Why?"

She waved my protests aside and lit up a cigarette.

"I don't usually talk about my private life, but I had a feeling that I'd like to talk to you. I'm not used to feeling like that, and so that I don't get a guilty conscience about bombarding you with my problems, I'd like to pay for dinner. Please accept."

My astonishment about the evening slowly died away. Right now, she looked very vulnerable.

"You really don't need to pay me to listen, but if you really want to treat me to dinner, then thank you. Even though, as I said, it's not necessary. I often needed someone to listen to me over the last few months. It really helps," I said.

The waiter came back with the ice cooler and wine and provided Luise with a distraction with the usual procedure of tasting and pouring. Once both wine glasses were full, I raised my glass and nodded to Luise.

"So, start."

Luise took a sip, a deep breath, and began. As she spoke, the clichés that I had built up in my mind about her disappeared one after another.

Her parents had separated when Luise was fourteen.

"It was like something from *War of the Roses*. My father is a teacher, a typical civil servant with all the accompanying principles. My mother worked in a boutique and as a fashion designer too. They were always arguing. And then, when she was almost forty, my mother fell in love with an Italian hotelier while we were on vacation together. So intensely that although she came back to Frankfurt with us, she ended up moving to Milan two months later. My father was furious."

She gave a pained smile. "I stayed living with my father, finished school in Frankfurt, and then went to study fashion design in Berlin."

Luise's father was as disapproving of Berlin as he was of her decision to study fashion. When she still hadn't come to her senses after two years, he cut her off financially.

I was appalled. "And what about your mother?"

Luise shrugged. "She stayed out of it, and I don't think she was too bothered. She's been in Milan for twenty-five years now and has burned all her bridges here. I sometimes visit, but after four days she gets on my nerves. We have very little in common."

Luise looked for a job. By chance she found one in a bookstore, and after half a year the owner offered her a training position. She accepted, and her interest in books overtook her interest in fashion.

"It was a wonderful time in my life. I was sharing an apartment with two of my colleagues, we got along well, the job was great, and then I fell in love too."

Dirk was a carpenter. He was renovating part of the bookshop and fell head over heels in love with Luise.

"I've never been wooed like that. It was like something in a movie. Every day he would bring something for me—sometimes a rose, sometimes a baguette for lunch, sometimes cinema tickets. We got along so well with each other, and everything was so easy with him. After my parents' marriage I hadn't even believed something like that could be possible."

After Luise ended her studies, Dirk began his. He wanted to become a schoolteacher, so Luise supported them both financially.

"That sounds familiar," I said. "It was exactly the same with us. Let me guess, while he was studying things were still great, but as soon as he finished, he changed."

Luise looked at me in surprise. She pushed her empty starter plate aside. We hadn't even paid any attention to the food.

"Exactly. When we moved to Hamburg eight years ago, everything was fine at first. Dirk loved it at his school, I became a rep, we got an apartment in Eppendorf. I thought things would just get better."

When the main course was served, we tried to pay more attention to it. It tasted delicious. With her mouth full Luise said, "Dirk hates fish."

I swallowed first and then answered, "Bernd hates expensive restaurants with small portions. He doesn't get it."

Luise continued with her story. It all sounded very familiar to me. Two different lives, held together by the bonds of many years and a shared daily routine. Friendly interaction without physical closeness. Shared plans for holidays and purchases as a way of proving to yourself that you have a future. Day by day, year by year, the same old routine.

Luise rubbed her eyes. "And then, two years ago, I was at the book fair. We had an event in a Frankfurt bar; I tipped over a glass of wine and met Alex. He's a press manager in Berlin. We talked the whole evening and the whole night, and then ended up in my hotel room."

I listened, fascinated.

The dessert plates lay before us, untouched. We were no longer hungry. Emotions can sometimes be very filling.

"To cut a long story short, we met up again. Two weeks later, when I was visiting my father. Then again when he had business in Hamburg. I've been having an affair for two years now. On the one hand it's wonderful, but on the other the guilt is destroying me."

I offered Luise one of my cigarettes.

"And now you want to leave Dirk?"

Luise looked at me sadly.

"I didn't want to at first. After all, Alex was with someone too, and we talked about the fact that neither of us wanted to separate from our partners. We just wanted to enjoy each other, have it as something special. But since February everything's turned upside down. Alex has left his partner, and although he said the decision wasn't just to do with me, I still feel under pressure."

"My separation was in February too."

I wasn't sure if I said it out loud or just thought it. Either way, Luise didn't pick up on it.

I touched her hand as she played with her lighter.

"So how can I help you now?"

"You've already helped me. I've never told anyone this before. Just looking at you helps me. You've got it all behind you now, and you look so good, and that makes me feel less scared."

I had the feeling I needed to set something straight, but I stayed silent.

"You know, Christine, despite all the difficulties, Dirk is my home, more of a home than I've ever had. If I stay, I have security. Perhaps love and passion aren't that important in the grand scheme of things. On the other hand, I can't begin to imagine my life without Alex. It would kill me."

She looked at me. Her mascara was smudged.

"It did me good to talk about it all. I hope I didn't offload on you too much."

I thought about Ines, Marleen, and Dorothea and smiled at her.

"That's what evenings like this are for. My friend Marleen said to me, 'In half a year's time you'll be laughing about it all.' My sister writes lists. You'll get through it in your own way, I'm sure of that."

Later, we walked to the cab line at the main station. Luise hugged me and whispered, "Thank you" in a voice that almost brought tears to my eyes. As I sat in the cab on my way home, I felt very happy to know Luise.

Relapse

snapped the lock shut on my suitcase and took a deep breath. In my hallway were two pilot cases, a box of sample texts, a box of paperwork, and my laptop bag. Everything I needed for the next three months was packed.

Over the last two weeks I'd confirmed my appointments, read manuscripts, compiled client lists, and put together samples folders. There were two trips a year. The first ran from January to April, the second from June to September. On each appointment in a bookshop the next one would be made, and that was how the schedule was arranged. It was my last evening of freedom; the next day would be the first of the new tour. I opened a bottle of red wine, took a glass from the cupboard, and sat down in the kitchen. My day planner lay on the table. I opened it and scanned through the appointments for the week to come.

It was a strange feeling.

I always used to visit the bookshops that were closest to me during the first week, going home each night. After that the stays in hotels began. The clients for next week were the same as I always had in the first week, but it wasn't a home game anymore. Now I'd have to stay with Marleen. When I'd arranged the appointments in January, I'd had no idea what would happen to me just five weeks later. I closed the day planner and put it in my briefcase. For the first time I'd be spending the night in the place that I'd fled from as fast as I possibly could.

Marleen had come to visit me the weekend before. She'd given me a house key with a bow tied around it. "I've renovated the guest room—yellow walls, blue bed, with a TV and a desk for your laptop. So you'll have your own room, your own bathroom, and now your own key as well. I'm really looking forward to us seeing more of each other. We can spend the evenings on the terrace having an after-work glass of champagne."

I had suppressed my thoughts of Bernd, Antje, my cats, the house, and neighbors and tried to share Marleen's enthusiasm. But now, the night before, the thoughts were back. I'd be spending three nights sleeping only ten minutes away from Bernd. It made me feel queasy.

Before the pictures could come to my mind, I stood up, fetched the telephone, and dialed Luise's number. We'd met up twice since the evening at Cox. By now she'd heard my story too and told me more about herself. There was a time when she used to make me feel intimidated. That time had gone, and she saw me as strong.

"Hi, Christine." She'd recognized my number on her display.

"Hi, Luise, I just wanted to wish you a great start to the tour."

"The same to you. Where are you starting?"

I named the places. She laughed.

"That's great, start off with your old hometown and then it'll be behind you. Put those fierce trousers on that you wore to Cox and treat it as a victory lap. You left a country bumpkin and you're coming back as a swan. That's really something."

I hadn't looked at it like that. She really did think I was strong. I wished I was. We made plans to have dinner the following weekend. I hung up the telephone, took my wine glass, and settled out on the balcony with a cigarette. I thought about the image that Luise had of me. Maybe she was right. My life was gradually getting some structure. All you had to do was figure out the beginning, and the rest would follow of its own accord.

I stubbed the cigarette out, looked at the time, went into the lounge, and turned the TV on. Sunday, eight fifteen. I was sure that millions of single women were watching *Law and Order* and painting their toenails. Just as I was. Bright red.

By the time I stopped in front of Marleen's house the next evening, I had the most demanding day of the tour behind me. It had been difficult to concentrate on the publishing program because the questions about my move to Hamburg came in every bookshop. Each time I gave a brief but friendly answer and tried to see myself through Luise's eyes. But as soon as I was back in the car to drive to the next appointment, the memories came flooding back. I'd met Antje in that café, that was the theatre I'd taken her children to for a Christmas pantomime, there was the Chinese restaurant where Bernd and I had celebrated buying our house. I drove past my old mechanic's, the vet's, the supermarket.

The weight of the memories became heavier and heavier. Somehow though, I made it through the day.

As my car stopped in front of Marleen's house, I realized how exhausted I was. My tears were ready to fall. I gritted my teeth and climbed out. Before I even had time to open the trunk, Marleen was standing before me with two filled glasses.

"If you drink a glass of champagne after the first day, it will bring you luck for the whole tour. Welcome."

She passed me a glass, beaming happily.

"It's wonderful to see you."

It did me a world of good to be welcomed like this. The tears retreated.

"Thank you, Marleen. It was a strange day, but it can only get better. Cheers."

As I unpacked my things in the guest room and hung my clothes in the wardrobe, I told her about the first day. Marleen sat on the bed, listened to me, and drank champagne. I pushed the empty travel bag under the bed and sat down next to her.

"These goddamn memories are really getting me down. It really isn't good to leave a place in shock, you know. It always catches up with you."

Marleen drank the glass empty and rotated it around in her hand.

"Of course, it's your first week back. Next time around it'll be easier. Come on, let's sit out on the terrace. I've made a lasagna and bought two really expensive bottles of red wine."

We went downstairs. At the bottom she turned around to me.

"By the way, what happened to your elbow and knee?"

I couldn't help but laugh. "Be discreet, otherwise I'll never tell you anything ever again."

After my first glass of red wine and a big helping of lasagna I felt much better. The terrace was surrounded by rose hedges and flowers, and the sun shone down warmly onto my back. Over dinner I told Marleen about the work gathering, the evening with Luise, and the last two weeks.

"When I think back on how every day was too long in those first weeks, I felt so overwhelmed and was terrified of falling over and only being found three days later. Do you remember? Yet in the last two weeks I've had so much to do with preparations for the tour. Nina came by, I went cycling with Eva and Judith, met Leonie to go shopping and then Luise too. All of a sudden it's working out."

Marleen poured more wine.

"And it's not even been half a year yet. Didn't I tell you?"

She looked up. "Is that a car I can hear?"

I'd heard it too. I recognized the footsteps on the garden path and the whistling. I flinched. Marleen had stood up and was looking around the corner. Her voice was expressionless.

"Hello, Bernd."

He came around the corner and stood before me. My hands were shaking. He leaned over and kissed me briefly on the cheek, smiling at me.

How familiar his face was.

"Christine, I've been trying to get hold of you on the phone for three weeks now, but every time I just get your answering machine. You're always out and about."

I stared at him and couldn't say a word. Marleen's voice sounded icy.

"Answering machines can record voices, you know. You could have left a message."

Bernd ignored her. "I'd like to speak to you in private." This was how he used to look at me.

Marleen cleared her throat. I awoke from my stupor and looked at her, nodding. She raised her shoulders in resignation and piled the plates and leftover lasagna onto a tray with a clatter, saying, "Fine, then I'll just clean up." Her body language clearly showed her hostility.

Bernd sat down on the chair opposite me and watched her go, shaking his head.

"Loyalty is all very well and good, but Marleen overdoes it a bit. I mean, she hasn't even offered me a drink."

I felt torn.

"She didn't invite you here, and besides, she knows what it's been like for me over the last months."

He looked at me for a while. "Well, you wouldn't know that things have been tough to look at you. You look good. New clothes?"

I was wearing the black blazer from Bremen. I looked at him again.

"What do you want to talk to me about?"

He pulled his chair nearer to me, took my glass, and drank from it.

"I thought our meeting with Hans-Hermann was dreadful. I felt really bad afterwards. After all, we had a great time together, and then suddenly we're sitting there like enemies and talking about accounts and money."

"Well, it wasn't me that started it all."

"Christine, I know that. Everything happened so badly; that wasn't what I wanted. I didn't mean for you to get hurt. We were always a good team, and we could still be one too."

I could feel myself losing the distance from him that had taken so much time and effort to build up.

He took my glass again and carried on talking.

"It's just seems ridiculous for us to break off contact. We could always meet up when you're working here, and I'd really love to see your place in Hamburg. But instead of that we're letting Hans-Hermann dissect our marriage into tiny pieces."

Our marriage. I looked at my hands. The narrow line that my wedding ring had left behind was nowhere to be seen, thanks to the Sylt sunshine. I thought about Jens.

Then I asked, "And what about Antje?"

"It's not what you think. It's just sex, that's all."

The distance came back.

"Christine! Don't look at me so coldly. We have to be able to get past this."

In need of air, I stood up abruptly. "I have to go to the bathroom. I'll be back in a moment."

Marleen was standing in the kitchen, stubbornly polishing glasses. "Who does that rat think he is?"

I put my hand on her shoulder, trying to calm her down.

"Don't get worked up. I think he's sorry about how it all happened."

"Who can believe that? No, either he wants money or he's up to something else. I wanted to talk to you about him anyway. Don't try to tell me he's been feeling bad about it all, you just wait."

Her rage surprised me. I took the glass and tea towel from her hand and pushed her in the direction of the front door. Before she reached it she turned around; I went back out onto the terrace. Bernd was just about to start talking again when Marleen walked up. Without a word, she put a glass by Bernd and sat down next to him.

He looked at her, confused.

She looked back. "What's the problem? I live here, you know."

I tried to figure out what was going on, but I knew there was something I didn't understand.

"Marleen, we're having a kind of peace talk. Your divorce was amicable, after all, and you still meet up with Adrian."

She reached for my cigarettes.

"That's because of the children, even if they are grown up now. And besides, Adrian wasn't so dishonest."

I felt as though she was going too far, and that I should defend Bernd.

He jumped in first. "Marleen, we've known each other for over twenty years now. It's very nice that you've helped Christine so much, but you shouldn't believe everything that people around here are saying about our separation."

She slammed her glass down on the table. I flinched. Then she turned towards Bernd and looked at him, her eyes narrowed.

"Okay, I didn't want to have to bring this up because I find it so unspeakable, but please! I ran into Inge and Frank at the bakery last week. We chatted, and I told Inge that Christine was going to be arriving today."

I listened to her, but I had no idea what our neighbors could possibly have to do with this. They hadn't been in touch since I left, even though I'd sent them a card with my new address. Bernd avoided making eye contact with me.

Marleen carried on, looking at me. "Inge reacted very strangely and said that she had no particular desire to see you."

I was surprised. "But why? I didn't do anything to them."

Marleen looked at Bernd with a strange expression, then back at me.

"Inge was shocked that you'd had a lover in Hamburg for the last two years without anyone knowing about it. And then you just picked up and left out of the blue to be with him. Bernd was just lucky that Antje was there to help him through such a difficult time, with the house and the gardening. After all, he couldn't manage it by himself."

I was speechless.

Marleen wasn't done with Bernd yet. "I'm sure Inge just got the wrong end of the stick, so I set her straight. And then I made sure a few other people knew the truth too."

Bernd looked at her stonily. "Are you done?"

"Yes, and now I feel sick to my stomach. I'm getting myself a brandy."

She stood up and left us alone.

"Bernd, what the hell have you done?"

"My God, Christine. It really doesn't matter why we separated, does it? I mean, no one's really interested. You just took off, and you're doing fine now, so whatever I do doesn't really matter to you."

"What on earth do you mean? How could it not matter?"

"You've got a new apartment, and you're earning good money, while I've got the whole house around my neck and on top of that have to pay you fifteen thousand euros. Because Hans-Hermann commanded it."

"But you've kept everything. You wanted the house. You wanted the separation. So why are you two lying to everyone?"

"Oh, don't be so stubborn. You can't just forgive, can you? Antje can't understand it either. This kind of thing happens all the time, and in a year's time everyone will have forgotten about it. You're the only one sulking."

Marleen had heard the last two sentences.

"Bernd, I want you to leave now. And quickly, before I really lose my temper."

I couldn't move or say a word.

I watched my husband as he ripped his car keys out of his jacket in a rage and went to his car. The brakes squealed as he sped away.

Marleen handed me a grappa.

"Get that down you."

I sat down and drank the glass empty. Everything felt like it was happening in slow motion. "I thought it couldn't get any worse."

Marleen poured me some more. "This really is the limit. But this is as bad as it's going to get. There's a reason behind everything. Bernd clearly overextended himself; he had no idea how much you were paying for. And Antje was being given the cold shoulder, so they came up with this story to explain it all. That's why no one has been in touch with you. But now I've put the story straight, and Antje will be the one with the problem, which she's sure to take out on Bernd. It's all so horrible."

"I'm not in the slightest bit sorry for them. I don't want to hear about it anymore."

My gaze wandered across the dark terrace. It was already late.

In my mind I saw Luise in Cox, Jens on the beach chair, my balcony, Dorothea waving to me.

Marleen was watching me. "Perhaps this whole drama has a silver lining. You were too soft; you weren't angry enough." I returned her gaze.

"Perhaps. I've no idea. At the moment I just feel numb. And cold."

In the middle of the night, I woke up. I switched the light on and sat up. Looking at the wall opposite, a framed photograph caught my eye that I hadn't noticed the day before.

Beach chairs on Sylt.

I opened the window, sat on the ledge, and smoked a cigarette. *Ten minutes away,* I thought, *what a load of crap.*

I lay back down in bed and turned out the light. Shortly before I fell asleep, a thought came into my mind. Maren's husband was a lawyer. I would give her a call. It was time.

At Any Price

Nina missed the ball by a hair's breadth and let out a load groan. She's panting just as much as me, I thought, wiping the sweat from my brow. Breathing heavily, Nina leaned against the wall and, sapped of energy, let her squash racket fall from her hand to the floor.

"Eight to five," I announced. "Come on, Nina, it's my match point."

She struggled to catch her breath and got into position.

"Go on. At least the game's nearly over. If I carry on much longer I'll be sick!"

She didn't even manage to return the serve.

As we sat opposite each other in the changing room, sweaty and breathless, Nina massaged her calf with a pained expression.

"I'm not sure whether squash is the right thing for my old body. I'm forty now...maybe I should just stick to going for walks."

I untied my sneakers. "We should just play more often, that's all. I hurt all over too, but it was really fun."

Nina pulled her T-shirt—emblazoned with the slogan "The Best of the North"—over her head and threw it in her sports bag. She pulled her hair out of its ponytail, looking at me.

"You've been playing for years, haven't you?"

For a moment I saw Antje before me in her sports gear.

"I used to play regularly with a girlfriend. But I haven't for the last year."

Antje and I used to meet up every other weekend to play squash, but in that last year she'd allegedly had problems with her knee and had cancelled again and again.

"Nina, you play well; you didn't exactly seem like a beginner either."

In the meantime she'd gotten out of her sweaty gear, wrapped a towel around herself, and picked up her shower things.

"Twenty years of tennis, that's enough. It didn't used to hurt so much."

She laughed and disappeared into the shower.

We'd bumped into each other in Bremen the week before. She was just coming out of a bookstore that I had my next appointment in. We both had half an hour to kill and went for coffee. She asked if I'd settled in well, and we talked about the journey, about the packed schedule of appointments.

"The thing that most annoys me is how sedentary the job is. You're sitting in the car all day, and with customers, and then at the desk or on the sofa in the evenings." Nina laid her cookie back on the saucer. "I'd love to take up sports again, but there's so little time in the week for training."

She looked at me. "Do you do anything?"

"Not at the moment, but I used to play squash."

She was immediately excited. "That's great, let's play together this weekend. I'll book us a court and pick you up."

She wrote it in her appointment book, snapped it shut contentedly, and ate the cookie.

Now we were sitting, freshly showered and with blow-dried hair, in the bar that belonged to the sports center. We could see the squash court below us through the tinted glass panes. Nina wrinkled her forehead and looked down. "Oh God, that means everyone could see me sweating away."

My gaze fell on two young girls, twenty at most, who were at least ten kilos overweight. They moved clumsily and slowly; it looked like it was their first squash session. "Well, take a look at those two. They're half our age and it seems like they've never played sports before."

Nina followed my gaze.

"My God, such spring chickens and so inflexible. We look an awful lot better than they do."

My arm was shaking from exertion, so much so that I had to hold my beer glass with both hands. Nina watched me, looking pleased.

"I'm glad I'm not the only one who's done in. But seriously, can we do it more often? I really enjoyed it."

I drank and put the glass back down. Only a few memories had come up while we played. I'd thought it would be much worse.

"I'd love to. It did me good."

For a few minutes we watched two men who were locked in an unbelievably quick volley on one of the courts. When they stopped, Nina turned back to me.

"Are you getting used to big city life?"

"Yes, little by little."

I didn't feel inclined to tell her about the dismal early days. Particularly as I still had dark moments now and then. She, on the other hand, seemed so self-confident and assured.

I wasn't expecting her next question. "Do you have a boyfriend?"

I looked at her, amazed. "I've only been separated for six months. I couldn't even imagine having one at the moment."

The two men had started playing again. They hit the balls with strength and impressive speed. I found their technique sensational, and I held my breath during a particularly difficult volley. The winner of the point raised his fist in victory.

Nina was watching, equally fascinated.

I got my breath back. "They're amazing. I've never seen anything like it."

Her facial expression was unreadable.

The game continued. Nina said something that was too quiet for me to hear. I asked her again.

"I said, they're probably married."

I was confused. "Who?"

Her look was earnest. "The two supermen, of course. Men like that are always married. You can forget about it."

"I meant I thought the *game* was amazing, not the men."

Nina raised her eyebrows. "Oh, okay, I misunderstood. Yes, you're right, they play well. Shall we pay, or do you want another one?"

"Let's go. I'm starting to get hungry."

Nina thought for a moment. "Okay, then how about we drive to my place. I'll show you where I live, you can meet my dog Edda, then we'll go to the Italian place around the corner; it's really good. What do you think? Fancy it?"

I did.

Nina lived in Altona in a loft—she'd already told me that. As we crossed through the courtyard that led to her apartment, I was already impressed by the exterior of the old factory building. High windows, lushly planted pots and a balcony, lots of glass and old stone. The apartment was just as impressive inside. Nina gestured to a seating area with her hand and went upstairs.

I'd only seen apartments like this on TV. On the last episode of *Law and Order* a famous film star was under suspicion of murder. The investigation had taken place in similar surroundings.

There was about 150 square meters of living space, divided between two floors. The kitchen was open-plan; I recognized the designer. My whole apartment would have fit in her bathroom.

I realized that my mouth was open.

Nina had come back, accompanied by a friendly looking German shepherd dog carrying something in its mouth. "May I introduce you? Christine, this is Edda. Edda, Christine."

The dog tilted her head to the side and gave a whimper.

I stroked her head. "Pleased to meet you, Edda. What's that you've got in your mouth?"

Nina pushed my hand away. "Christine, don't take that away from her. It's the muffler."

"What?"

Edda whimpered and looked at me with her loyal eyes.

"She's always so happy when visitors come, and she barks like crazy. When she was still a puppy, I got so annoyed on my birthday one time that I stuffed a couple of rolled-up socks in her mouth. That was the first time I didn't scold her when visitors were here. With the socks, the barking just became a whimper. Anyway, at some point she must have noticed that I didn't shout at her anymore when she got excited. So now, when she hears the door, she fetches the socks right away. And whimpers."

I started to laugh.

Edda looked at me, wagging her tail and continuing to whimper. My laughter started Nina off, and we could hardly control ourselves. Still whimpering, Edda rolled over on her back.

A little later, Nina wiped the tears from her eyes and blew her nose.

"I could always order takeout from the Italian restaurant; then I wouldn't have to leave Edda alone again so soon."

By now, the dog had calmed down and spat the socks out. After two short barks, looking at Nina, she sat down in front of me and laid her head on my knee. I found Edda captivating.

After Nina had ordered two pizzas with rocket and Parma ham, she opened a glass of red wine, put glasses on the table, and sat down on a chair opposite me. I couldn't hold my question back any longer.

"Tell me, Nina, it's perhaps a little indiscreet of me to ask, but how much do you have to earn to be able to live like this?"

She laughed and looked at me briefly. "I don't have to earn it. The apartment belongs to me; it's my divorce settlement."

I really did pick the wrong man, I thought to myself.

Nina poured the wine and carried on talking.

"I was with my ex-husband for twenty years in total, and we were married for fifteen of those. We lived in Kiel; Karsten studied there and then started working in the university clinic. I worked in the bookstore. We had a house together, were in a tennis club, went on vacation twice a year—everything was wonderful."

She took a sip of wine. Her face became hard all of a sudden.

"Then I found out that Karsten was having an affair with one of his colleagues. I didn't actually mind, and so I didn't say a word. I didn't want anything to change."

I listened to her, gripped. My own story was becoming less and less original.

Nina looked at me, and there was an angry furrow between her eyes.

"I'm not naïve. Of course the initial intensity is gone after twenty years, but that's not what it's about. It was my life. I liked the house, our circle of friends, our daily life. As I said, I didn't want to change anything. But then his fancy woman got pregnant; Karsten had to tell me about it and said he wanted a divorce. He never wanted children. But she was determined. I mean really, a doctor and no idea about contraception! I don't think it was Karsten's idea to leave me."

I had an uneasy feeling. "Are they still together?"

Nina snorted. "They've got a practice together now, and they got married because of that. They don't fit together at all. I'll be interested to see how long it lasts."

"How long have you been divorced?"

"The last five years."

Before I could answer, the delivery man from the Italian restaurant rang the doorbell.

We sat down at the table. For a while we ate in silence. Then Nina suddenly asked, "How did we get onto all that?"

I thought about it. "Oh yes, the apartment being a divorce settlement."

"Right."

Nina smiled contentedly as she talked. "My brother-in-law is a lawyer, so we really put the pressure on Karsten when it came to the divorce. I got a test to say I couldn't work anymore for psychological reasons, and that he had to support me. We didn't have a prenup. He wasn't happy about it. But I wasn't prepared to let my standard of living go down the drain just because that idiot was fucking around. So we took him for everything he had, and in the end he had to pay me one big lump sum. For tax reasons he bought this apartment and wrote it over to me. That's all there was to it."

I pushed my plate aside, leaving half the pizza uneaten. I wasn't hungry anymore.

I tried to change the subject.

"When I first moved to Hamburg I wanted to give you a call, to get tips about single life here. You seem to have everything under control. But I lost my nerve."

Nina looked at me in astonishment and then laughed bitterly.

"Me? I hate single life. The apartment's too big for me, and I only ever meet married men who sleep with me a few times and then go back to their wives. I answer personal ads and meet men who want to have their fun but no relationship, and the men I get to know on club holidays I never hear from again. I've had enough of it, Christine, just enough! I want to be woken up in the morning by a man kissing me, not from the noise my dog makes when she throws up."

I was shocked by her outburst and searched for something to say.

Nina must have been just as shocked as me. She smiled, embarrassed, and said quickly, "And my dog throws up a lot."

I forced myself to smile. The embarrassed silence was broken by the telephone ringing. Nina spoke to her office quickly and then came back; saying with a shrug of her shoulders, "I'm sorry, that was my friend who normally looks after Edda when I'm away. She usually picks her up, but she can't today because she has a visitor. I have to drive Edda there."

I was relieved at the unexpected end to the evening.

"Nina, I'm ready to turn in myself. Thank you for the meal and the game of squash. Let's talk on the phone. I'll get the train; it'll be quicker."

I was happy to shut the door behind me. And yet I felt guilty for feeling that. I heard Edith's voice.

Don't be like that; you'll get to that stage too. Just you wait, before long you'll be just as desperate for a man as she is.

Charlotte held her own.

Nonsense, you never had it so good in the last years with Bernd as you do now. You're completely different from her.

I hoped she would turn out to be right.

Dirty Money

A fat old woman raised her liquor glass to the camera. She gave a toothless, happy grin, while a speech bubble proclaimed, "You did it!"

I turned the card over. "Today is August 11. The half year is up. Best wishes, Marleen."

What a sweetheart. She had remembered.

I laid the card on the pile of mail, shut the mailbox, and climbed up the stairs to my apartment. It was Friday at lunchtime; I was home early and had the whole weekend ahead of me. With my first customer this morning I'd written the date on the order form. August 11. That's when I realized.

It was behind me now, the first six months that I'd feared so much back in February. I should really celebrate somehow. As I got into my apartment I put my bag in the office, emptied a box of business mail onto the desk, and laid the small pile from the mailbox next to it.

I stuck the card from Marleen onto the fridge. The fat old woman toasted me as I opened it. It was actually much too early, but the last half year had been something out of the ordinary. I took a small bottle of champagne out. I had bought it for a special occasion. And that was now.

As I sat on the balcony and toasted myself, I felt almost daring—and proud and relieved all at the same time.

Charlotte smiled at me.

Congratulations. You're a wonderful woman.

I thought of Nina; she wouldn't know this feeling. She'd only be relieved when she could introduce the new man in her life. We had continued to play squash, but we confined our get-togethers to that and a post-match beer. Her bitter search for a man depressed me, and I had declined her invite to accompany her to singles parties. When I laughed after she'd described the "Fish seeks bicycle" party to me, she'd seemed put out.

As long as I managed to keep her away from the subject of men, I liked her.

Edith had a go.

You're both alone on the weekends.

I didn't want to listen to her. Perhaps I should invite Luise to dinner. She still had this first half year ahead of her. Three weeks ago she had stood in front of my door, even slimmer than usual, with eyes swollen from crying. "I didn't know where to go. Can I come in?" We sat in the kitchen late into the night drinking red wine.

Luise had tried for weeks to figure out her feelings for Dirk, whom she lived with, and Alex, whom she longed for. She had booked a weekend away at Hidden Lake and surprised Dirk with it.

"We used to go there all the time when we were first together, deeply in love, and always flat broke. It was always amazing. I wanted to do everything I could to be sure that I still wanted to live with Dirk. I thought I could get that old magic back."

They didn't find the old magic. Instead, they spent the weekend pretty much in silence.

Luise smoked one cigarette after the other. "I tried desperately to find things we had in common, but all we had are common habits. We had a few forced conversations about people we knew, exchanged banal tidbits of conversation. We had time for each other and no idea what to do with it. Can you imagine that?"

I could, and I poured her some more wine.

Luise drank and kept talking. "In the evenings we couldn't even bring ourselves to have sex. I wouldn't have been able to anyway. And then, suddenly, we started talking. Dirk accused me of having changed. He said he couldn't understand me anymore. He asked whether I still loved him, and I suddenly realized that I didn't. He looked at me and knew it was over. And then he cried."

The tears were running down Luise's face now.

"I felt so guilty about Alex, and I was sad because Dirk was so sad. We drove back this morning. He was the first one to mention the word 'separation.' As soon as it was out, I felt both distraught and relieved."

I pushed a new pack of tissues towards her. "What has Alex said about it?"

She looked at me, her eyes red. "I haven't told him yet. We haven't seen each other for four weeks, and I didn't want to just tell him on the phone. I want to get my own place first and then see what happens."

She slept on my sofa while I lay awake in my bed, uncomfortably reminded of the night I'd spent at Ines's. Starting all over again from the beginning, I thought, and then I pushed the thought away. It wasn't my story this time; I was further on.

I'd recently met up with Maren and her husband Rüdiger, the lawyer. We went out to dinner; the evening was relaxed and long. We talked about books, films, travel, and eventually, about my marriage. I described the last few years and tried to leave out my feelings. A few days later I had an appointment at Rüdiger's office. I brought with me the documents from Hans-Hermann, which Rüdiger scanned through, frowning.

"So, Christine, if I understood you right, you don't want the house, your husband wants to take over all the loans, you want out of everything so that you're not tied to any of it, and apart from the settlement of fifteen thousand euros that he's paid you, you don't have any more demands?"

I nodded. "I just want out. And I don't want to pay anything for him anymore; I've been doing that for years. The house is encumbered with the mortgage, so if he pays it off alone, that's fine by me."

Rüdiger shook his head slightly.

"Other couples fight over every last eggcup, so this'll be an easy divorce. And you're sure that fifteen thousand euros is enough for the things you've left there?"

I took a deep breath. "It's enough. Hans-Hermann calculated it. But Bernd hasn't paid me yet. I thought that was only due when the divorce goes through."

Rüdiger looked up, confused. "Why hasn't he paid yet? It's an indemnity payment, just like you would pay a previous tenant. You should have received it immediately after moving out. Then the divorce will cost less too. That was what was arranged."

I thought about my last conversation with Bernd. And I heard Marleen saying, "Bernd clearly overextended himself."

I felt overwhelmed.

Rüdiger seemed to notice. "You told us at dinner that you don't want to argue about money, and I can accept that. But you shouldn't be just giving things away either. I'll write him a letter and take care of it—you don't need to worry."

He talked me through the divorce process. I felt sure that this is how I wanted things to happen. Everything was taking its course; I had a lawyer who knew his stuff, he was taking charge of the situation, and I felt relieved.

As I poured the rest of the champagne, I thought about Luise again. I was meeting her this evening. She'd asked me to go along with her to view an apartment. I drank my glass empty and looked at the time. In four hours she would be arriving to pick me up, but first I wanted to go through my mail. In my champagne-fuelled mood I wasn't particularly excited about the prospect, but I made a start anyway.

An hour later all my orders were ready, and the pile of mail was, apart from three slim envelopes, all gone. I hadn't changed my bank details yet, so I still received all my account statements in the mail. I stared at the last line of my private account statement in disbelief: 16,125.20 euros in credit. I'd never had a balance like that on any of my statements.

Rüdiger had sent me a copy of his letter to Bernd. He'd simply given Bernd my account number and asked him to transfer the agreed sum to the account. Apprehensively, I'd waited for Bernd's inevitable phone call, but it never came. Bernd's tendency to put off unpleasant tasks had annoyed me during our marriage too. He seemed to ignore bills, never took them seriously. We could have paid for a spa weekend with all the late fees I'd had to pay on his behalf over the years. And yet now he'd transferred the money.

Edith's voice was scornful.

It's dirty money.

Charlotte was pleased.

So what? Now you can pay Georg back, and you'll still have ten thousand euros left over. You'll be able to have some savings—finally!

I'd had a bad conscience for years that I never saved enough money. Bernd and I had taken on too much through his studies and buying the house, so we were just happy when we weren't heavily overdrawn, which had been a rare occurrence. And now this.

16,125.20 euros.

I was dizzy with happiness.

Charlotte was still thinking.

Of course, you could spend some of it as well. You've never been shopping without being cautious about the prices. Just one shop, perhaps the small jeweler in the Lange Reihe.

I had stood in front of the window a lot recently with the gnawing desire to buy myself a ring. After ten years of wearing a wedding ring, my hand looked lonely somehow, abandoned. The ring that I liked was on display in the window. There was no price on it.

Edith was incensed.

A ring. For that kind of money you could buy something sensible. You haven't even got a proper lamp in the bedroom yet, or a proper desk chair, but you'd buy a ring. Ridiculous.

My cell phone ringing interrupted my thoughts.

"Hello, Christine, it's Luise. I was just wondering, would you be able to make it a little earlier? The real estate agent just phoned, and she's already in the apartment, so we could look at it right now."

"Sure. I'm at home and I'm free. Where is it exactly?"

"I'm ten minutes from you, so I'll pick you up. Great! I'll see you soon."

Her voice sounded good.

As she drove into the parking space, I was standing by the front door with the account statement in my coat pocket.

The apartment was closer to mine than I'd thought. We only drove for ten minutes before turning off into a small side street. Luise wrinkled her forehead as she looked at the cars parked to the left and right.

"It's number fifteen, so if we get a space directly in front of the house, that'll be good luck."

As we found the house, a white delivery van put its lights on. Luise let it drive out, and then she pulled into the space. Laughing, she looked at me.

"Christine, it's a sign. God, please let the apartment be nice."

"And please let Luise get it." I climbed out and waited until she'd locked the car. She turned to me.

"No, that won't be a problem. I'll be able to get it. The owner is one of my mother's old customers, and I've known her for a while. So the apartment just needs to be nice."

Together, we walked up to the entrance. It was a white Art Nouveau villa, very well kept, with stucco molding and a small balcony.

Luise rang the doorbell, waited to be buzzed in, and looked at me.

"If it's as beautiful inside as out, then I hope it all works out. I don't want to keep looking; this is the fourteenth viewing already."

The buzzer unlocked the door, and I pushed it open.

"Well, fourteen brings good luck—that's old Tasmanian folklore."

"What?" Luise followed me, confused.

"It's good luck. Every fourteenth apartment brings good luck. Just believe it."

The stairwell was old and restored, with blue-green tiles, wooden banisters, and beautiful doors with brass handles. On the third floor, an apartment door opened. A blonde woman stepped out into the hall, with a fake smile, lots of makeup and hairspray, white trousers, pink jacket, and positively dripping with gold jewelry.

She shook Luise's hand, and her voice immediately went an octave higher. If you were playing some game to guess people's professions and the contestants were blindfolded, they would still be able to tell that this strange creature was a real estate agent. Her voice was horrendous.

"Wonderful, and this must be the girlfriend who's coming along for safety reasons. So delightful to meet you."

Her bracelets jangled. I was certain that she drove a BMW cabriolet.

Edith said, *What a stupid old mare.*

I smiled, gave her my hand, and felt slightly annoyed that I was yet again wearing the black blazer and that my jeans weren't completely clean. She would have noticed that right away, I was sure.

Charlotte reminded me, *You've got 16,125.20 euros to your name.*

I grasped the agent's hand tightly and gave a smile even wider than hers. She winced a little and quickly let my hand fall.

"Shall we?"

The apartment was made for Luise. Three large rooms, lots of daylight, and completely renovated. The real estate agent, who had introduced herself as Jeanette, could hardly contain her excitement about the faucets, the arrangement of the wall sockets, and the double-glazed windows, her voice becoming ever more shrill.

Luise walked through the rooms with her usual long stride, gave Jeanette a long look, and then interrupted her with a soft but firm voice.

"It's good. Thank you. I'll take it."

Jeanette closed her mouth.

"Oh, okay, that's great, wonderful, but shouldn't I explain the kitchen appliances to you first? They're so wonderful…"

"No." Our voices came in unison.

A little hurt, she promised Luise that she would send her the rental contract in the next few days and clarified the dates. The apartment would be ready beginning next week, and she could move in then. She let us go ahead and then made an elaborate show of locking the front door. As we walked through the lobby, she pointed out the blue-green tiles and wooden banisters to us. I looked at the door signs to the other apartments while Luise looked at Jeanette politely. As we arrived downstairs, her voice was just as shrill as it had been upstairs. She threw her small pink jacket on the back seat of a red BMW cabriolet, climbed in, waved at us cheerfully, and roared off.

Luise looked at me, I looked at her, and then we started to laugh. For minutes on end. About Jeanette, about the wonderful faucets, about BMW cabriolets, about shrill voices, and because Luise had a great apartment.

We wiped away our tears of laughter. "So, let's go and drink some champagne to toast my new home."

I looked in my bag for the crumpled bank statement. "Luise, it's my treat. Look at the figure right at the bottom."

She smoothed the statement out, looked, and then raised her eyebrows.

"What's this? Ah, Bernd? Christine, you've got some serious dough there. Let's go shopping tomorrow. I need some things anyway, so let's drive out to Stilwerk, that concept design store. We'll make a day of it."

She handed me back the statement, poked me in the side, and smiled.

"We've done it! At least, I almost have. There are good times ahead. I can feel it."

To me, her eyes looked sad. I hoped she wasn't thinking the same thing about me.

Retail Therapy

Bernd was walking in front of me. I looked at the hairline at the back of his neck and suddenly felt the enormous desire to touch him there, to kiss him. At that moment he stopped and turned around towards me, smiling. I felt his lips on my temple, heard his voice.

"I'm so happy you're back. I was such an idiot; I don't want to be without you."

My heart beat faster, and a feeling of security washed over me. I laid my hand on his cheek, tried to look into his eyes, and then heard the alarm clock.

Please, no, I thought, turning the alarm off. I stayed lying on my back for a moment and felt the cozy feeling disappear as I slowly woke up.

I heard Edith say, *He left you; he's fine without you. You were just dreaming.*

I shut my eyes again, saw Bernd's smile, felt his hands, felt the longing, and then felt lonely.

Charlotte tried to help. *You've got plans with Luise. You've got enough money; go shopping, buy something beautiful for your apartment. There'll be no one there to argue with anything, and it'll be a great day.*

Edith persisted. *It'll just be compulsive shopping to hide the loneliness. Never mind, that's what lots of women your age do; it's a kind of replacement life.*

I sat up, feeling dizzy. My back ached, and the feeling I'd had in my dream was still lingering. Bernd's voice was in my ear. "I don't want to be without you." I was annoyed to feel the tears coming, so I struggled out of bed and went into the bathroom.

Shortly before eleven a.m. I was standing outside the entrance to Stilwerk, waiting for Luise. It was an impressive building directly on the harbor. Modern architecture on the outside, and inside a collection of designer stores with furniture, fabrics, baths, decorations, and everything you could need to furnish an apartment in an old building so it looks like something from *House Beautiful.*

I'd come here five years ago with a colleague. We'd had a work meal nearby, and afterwards he'd asked if I could drive him to the station, but he had wanted to stop off and buy a showerhead on the way. I'd agreed and let him direct me to Stilwerk. In my naïveté I'd expected a DIY store and was speechless in awe as we stood in a small shop and he bought a showerhead that cost just as much as my entire bathroom had in the house. A DIY store indeed! Back then I had felt like I was in a different world here.

Charlotte reminded me again, *16,125.20 euros. Today you're part of it.*

I felt my anticipation mount.

I stepped aside to make room for a couple making their way towards the entrance. He let her go first, laying his hand on her back. She turned to him and smiled, stopped and kissed him, and then carried on. The revolving door separated them for a brief moment, but when he was set free, moments after she was, her hand was already waiting for his.

My gaze followed them.

Edith said, *You want that too.*

Charlotte answered, *They'll soon be squabbling because he thinks everything she likes is too expensive or just can't stand it.*

I didn't believe her and saw the waiting hand before me.

"Why are you making a face like that?" Suddenly, Luise was standing in front of me. She hugged me.

I shook the picture of the couple from my mind and looked at her. "I was lost in thought."

"Not particularly happy ones by the look of it."

She pulled me into the foyer of Stilwerk and looked around her.

"Isn't it insane? I love these shops. And even if we just look, it's still great."

Her enthusiasm swept the clouds from my mind.

Charlotte followed up: *16,125.20 euros. And no one who'll stick their oar in and want justifications.*

I took a deep breath, looked Luise up and down, noticed how thin she was, and said, "Shall we get some breakfast first and make a plan? Like what we're looking for?"

I steered her towards a small bistro right next to the entrance. We got a table by the window with a view over the Elbe and ordered two continental breakfasts from the ridiculously handsome waiter.

From here we could see right out over the parking lot, where more and more cars were arriving. I was surprised to see how many people could afford to spend their Saturdays shopping in Stilwerk. Luise's gaze followed mine. "Most of them are just looking." She toasted me with her coffee cup. "We can buy."

I felt a little excited and very lighthearted.

Luise took a scrap of paper from her handbag, pushed her bitten-into roll to the side, laid the list on the table, and smoothed it out.

"So, I need…"

Without stopping chewing, I took the note, pushed her plate back towards her, and said, somewhat imperceptibly, "Finish your breakfast first."

Luise looked at me. "What's up with you? You sound like my mother."

"I don't want you to get so thin that I look fat next to you. The handsome waiter will end up feeling sorry for the beautiful woman's fat friend. And I can't take pity."

Luise laughed and shook her head. "You're being silly."

She carried on eating while I scanned her list. Bed, bathroom mirror, lamps, rubbish bin, doormat.

I looked up, thought about the labels and prices here, and handed the list back to her.

"You do realize that you could get everything on that list in IKEA or the DIY store for a fraction of the price you'll end up paying here?"

She put the list back in her bag. "I know, that's what I always used to do. But I've got savings for bad times." She took a deep breath. "And I think that these aren't particularly good times. I'm furnishing an apartment for just myself, and I want it to be beautiful. I don't want to be sensible anymore, at least not today."

I thought about my new sofa and the other new things. And about how liberating it had felt to replace my old life with them.

"I bought a lot of new things too. Although the sofa was the only really extravagant thing; the rest was sensible. It doesn't really heal the pain, but it plasters the soul, so you can't see the hurt right away. And that definitely does you good."

Luise stubbed her cigarette out and beckoned the handsome waiter.

"Christine, we're not being sensible today, and I don't want any more sad feelings. Come on, let's go plaster our souls."

We made a start in a shop for bathroom fittings. It was the one I already knew. Baths made from wood, chrome, and porcelain, round and corner bathtubs, crazy wash-basins, and wild fittings. Along with decorations whose price tags made me gulp.

After twenty minutes Luise had chosen and reserved a bathroom mirror with a heavy silver frame. She looked very happy indeed. So did the man at the checkout counter.

I bought a soap dish made of blue porcelain, three chrome boxes, a shallow black basket, and a shower curtain. It came to 320 euros. A bargain, really. The elegant bag and my feeling of elation confirmed the feeling of foolishness that was growing within me.

Next up, a fabric store. We touched every fabric bauble, every fold, and found the colors beautiful. I looked at Luise. "I can't even sew."

She shrugged her shoulders regretfully. "Me neither."

"It's such a shame."

We left the store without any bags. The next one was an office equipment store. We sat on at least twenty office chairs, stroked our hands across writing tables, and turned lamps on and off. I bought a wall clock, three filing boxes, a container for paperclips, a table lamp, and a metal notice board—340 euros.

Luise picked up some catalogues.

Then there was a kitchen shop. Luise piled cups in her shopping baskets while I looked for candleholders and serviettes. We stopped for a while in front of the glasses. Luise picked up a red wine glass and looked at it admiringly; it was simple, big, beautiful.

"Look, Christine, this costs almost ten times as much as my glasses from IKEA."

She put a box of six in her basket. Next, we found ourselves looking at the espresso machines. These had been the epitome of a luxury kitchen to me for years. Bernd didn't like espresso; I loved it. Ines had once bought me a small pot for the stove; a machine was just a dream.

Luise stood next to me. "Which one are you getting?"

Charlotte whispered, *You've still got over ten thousand euros.*

My newfound reason beat Edith to it.

"Oh, it's not worth it. For just a few cups of espresso or cappuccino? Besides, none of them cost less than eight hundred euros."

Luise nudged me and laughed. I looked at her.

"Are you serious?"

"Christine, it's for you—of course it's worth it."

I saw myself standing in my bathrobe and warm socks in front of this wonderful chrome appliance in the mornings, saw myself push a button, heard the sound of the grinder, and smelled the coffee. The last bit turned out to be real; a shop assistant was standing in front of us, balancing two small red espresso cups.

"May I offer you an espresso and show you the machines?"

Half an hour later I was writing my address on the delivery paperwork and signing a credit card receipt for 1,150 euros. The candlesticks, serviettes, six espresso cups, chrome jug for hot milk, and a pepper grinder were an additional 160 euros. Luise got a dark gray material bag to carry her wine glasses and cups in. I felt great and grabbed her elbow.

"Luise, I've got an espresso machine. This is amazing. Let's have a break; I've got a completely dry throat."

We found a small bistro with standing tables and bar chairs, and we ordered a big bottle of water and two glasses of champagne. I was still over the moon; Luise laughed and raised her glass.

"To cappuccino and espresso and the fact that everything that we do for ourselves is worth it."

I was almost dizzy with happiness and drank some water to help calm myself down.

Charlotte was happy too. *An espresso machine. At last.*

Edith answered. *That's over two thousand euros you've spent on things that you don't really need. Call it a day now; you really need to put some money away.*

Luise interrupted both their voices. "What are you thinking about?"

I answered quickly. "Nothing, I'm just happy. Now let's find you a bed, and I'll take a look around."

Luise pulled her list back out of her bag. Before she could say a word, someone stumbled against our table and the water bottle fell over, spilling its contents directly between my elegant shopping bags and Luise's feet.

"Oh heavens, I'm so sorry. Oh God, is everything wet? I'm so terribly sorry. Oh, it's you guys. I didn't even recognize you. Well, isn't this great?"

Anke. Black miniskirt, tight top, poison-green jacket, red shoes, everything too tight, as usual. Her hair was crazy and wild, her face glowing.

She whirled off, said something to the waiter, and then ran over to a blond man who looked about thirty years old and talked on and on at him energetically. His handsome face looked pained.

Luise's facial expression was unfathomable.

I looked at her questioningly. She lowered her voice as one of the waiters dried our table with a cloth, and said, "Hamburg is a metropolis with more than 1.7 million inhabitants. This is the smallest bar in Stilwerk. And yet we still manage to run into Anke."

By now Anke was standing in front of our table with the young man in tow. He clearly didn't seem very comfortable. Luise's face still showed no discernible signs of emotion. I had no idea what was coming. I hardly knew Anke; I'd barely seen her outside of our gatherings. Anke pulled the young man nearer to her, looked first at him, then at us, and then introduced him with her usual loud voice.

"Girls, this is the lovely David. Isn't he delicious? And these are my colleagues, Luise and Christine."

Luise raised her eyebrows. David went red, and I felt incredibly embarrassed by Anke's behavior. In an attempt to save the situation I stretched my hand out to him, a little overdramatically perhaps, and said, "Hi, I'm Christine."

He shook my hand, which seemed to make him even more embarrassed.

Anke was unmoved. She stroked his blond locks and said, "So you're on a spree at Stilwerk? Are you girls earning too much, or what?"

She giggled. David carefully freed his shoulder from her grip. I searched for a noncommittal answer, but Luise beat me to it.

"Exactly." She waved to the waiter. "We'd like to pay please. And we still have a lot on our list. I'll just pop around the corner again, and then we have to push on. So, Anke, David, I hope you have a good day."

She stood up, nodded to them both briefly, and disappeared in the direction of the restroom. Anke looked at me, astounded.

"She's getting more and more arrogant. Christine, I really don't understand why you hang around with her."

I tried to catch my breath and find an answer, but David saved me. "Come on, Anke, we have to be at the fish restaurant on the harbor at twelve."

He smiled at her with effort, and she looked up at him with a smile that was equally forced.

"Oh yes, we must dash." She patted my shoulder. "Enjoy the rest of your shopping then, Christine. How's single life treating you? Well, hopefully it won't be forever. But keep your head up until then."

I didn't need to answer. David pulled her towards the exit, and she didn't turn around again. Luise came back to the table at the same time as the waiter and the bill. I already had the money in my hand. After I'd paid, I looked at Luise, who was putting her cigarettes in her bag and standing up.

"So who was that?" I asked.

Luise shrugged her shoulders. "That was so typical of Anke. Always making things embarrassing, always putting her foot in it and then blaming other people. I can't bear her."

I was astonished at the harshness of her reaction. "Oh, she's not that bad. I felt a bit sorry for that David. Is he her boyfriend? What happened to Werner?"

Luise rolled her eyes.

"Boyfriend! That's her new trophy. She's always picking up men, and they seem to get younger and younger. David must be ten years younger than her, easily. She makes out she's just some scatty woman and spends her whole time messing around with these boys. Completely brazen and always so that Werner gets wind of it. Then she complains about Werner and plays the innocent wife. And Werner and the others go along with her games. It's really messed up."

I was surprised. "How do you know about all this?"

By now we were walking up to the entrance of a furniture shop. Luise stopped.

"I know Werner from way back, from Berlin. I was friends with both of them. At the beginning of their marriage at least. But the whole story got more and more hypocritical and embarrassing, so I've all but broken off contact. Christine, I'll tell you another time; I'm not in the mood right now to let Anke ruin our day."

We were standing in front of the entrance. The door opened as I stood in front of the motion sensor. I went through and turned back to face Luise. At that moment her cell phone rang. She searched frantically through her bag, found it after the third ring, and took the call with an eager look on her face.

"Oh, hello, Franziska." She looked disappointed.

"No, you're not interrupting anything. I'm at Stilwerk with Christine. What can I do for you?"

She listened for a moment.

"They belong to…yes, exactly. Wait a moment, she's called Mrs. Strehlke, the one that buys the children's books too."

While Luise listened to Franziska, she smiled.

"You know, we were planning to window-shop, but Christine is going crazy in here, spending money left, right, and center. I know, just imagine."

Franziska was saying something. Luise looked at me.

"You think five hundred euros is an awful lot? Wait, Christine, what are you up to so far?"

I did a few quick sums and said, "Two thousand six hundred and twenty euros."

"Did you hear that, Franziska? Two thousand six hundred and twenty euros." She burst into loud laughter. "Yes, I'll tell her. Okay, I hope the rest of your work goes well. Bye."

Luise put her cell back in her bag, still smiling.

"Franziska reckons you'll get to ten thousand easily; after all, it's only midday. And she wanted me to remind you that expensive things don't save lives, but they can make them a damn sight nicer."

Make a note of that, Edith, I thought.

Luise's expression had relaxed again. But I couldn't help asking, "You were waiting for another call, weren't you?"

She shrugged her shoulders. "For some reason I'm always waiting for Alex to get in touch. But he hasn't. We haven't seen each other for weeks; we've only spoken on the phone. I wanted to sort out everything with Dirk first."

"Does he know that you've got your own place and are moving out?"

Luise bit her lip. "I sent him a text. His answer was, 'Give me time.'"

I felt compassion for her. "Oh, that's not great perhaps, but come on, you've got a great apartment, we're here now, and it will all work out somehow. After all, you had a good thing going, so maybe he means something else or he's really busy at the moment or he just mistyped. Just wait and see. It's easy to misunderstand these stupid text messages."

I hoped I was right.

Luise nodded. "Yes, hopefully. So, come on, I'll buy myself a huge bed and think of Alex, or the other men that will come after him."

We made our way slowly down the aisles. I decided not to let myself be intimidated and made an effort to put on a facial expression that left no doubt that I'd been shopping exclusively in shops like this for years. I thought about the sofa in the old house, wooden with red upholstery, 380 euros from IKEA, and the pinewood table in front of it, 120 euros from the Home Depot. Bernd had thought they were sensible purchases, and back then I thought we would buy something nicer later. Now it was later, and Antje was sitting on it.

Charlotte said, *Exactly, later is now, so buy yourself something beautiful.*

And at that moment I saw the most amazing armchair I had ever seen in my life. It was enormous, soft, warm, safe, dark red, velvety, and with a matching footstool. I went over to it, sat down, and felt like I never wanted to stand up again. I shut my eyes and heard Charlotte say, *Oh, yes,* and then Luise said, "I was looking for you. You wanted to look at the beds with me, right?"

I opened my eyes and looked at her. "I've just fallen in love. I have to have it, without a doubt."

Edith's voice said, *Only if it costs less than three hundred euros.*

Luise looked at me in it. "It really suits you. It's beautiful. How much does your new love cost then?" She looked for the price tag, shaking her head.

"This shop is too expensive for them to stick labels on the furniture. But it has to be somewhere."

She continued looking. I stood up and found a discreet price list on a small side table. "Luise, I've found it, four hundred and fifty euros. Sold!"

Charlotte was pleased. *That's fine. Give or take a hundred and fifty.*

I sat down contentedly and joyfully in the wonderful chair. Wrinkling her forehead, Luise studied the list. "You have to read it properly, sweetie. The footstool is four hundred and fifty, but that's without the velvet cover; with, it's six hundred and fifty. As I said, just for the footstool. The chair in velvet, so, just as you see it now, costs two thousand two hundred euros."

I swallowed. So did Edith. *Are you crazy? Almost three thousand euros? You paid that for half the kitchen in the old house.*

Charlotte answered, *Exactly, and now Antje is cooking in it.*

A very smart sales assistant popped up in front of us and smiled at me. His name tag said *Daniel.* "It's a really beautiful piece of furniture. Once you sit in it, you really don't want to get up again, do you?"

I smiled back and felt understood. Luise looked at me and opened her mouth. I was quicker.

"I'll take it."

Luise closed her mouth again.

The smart Daniel looked at me, baffled. He seemed disappointed that he couldn't do his sales pitch. Still sitting in my "half kitchen," I smiled up at him. I felt unbelievably good. He turned to Luise, appealing for help.

"Yes, er, okay."

She held his gaze. "And I need a bed."

Now he was really unsure. "If I may, er, show you something…"

Luise interrupted him. "I've already found one; come with me." She turned around and walked purposefully towards a huge bed, a dream in white, on which countless cushions and blankets were draped.

Before I followed Luise, I stroked the velvety arm of my new sanctuary. Daniel was watching me uncertainly and followed us. We stopped in front of the dream bed, where Luise was already laid out on her back. She spread her arms out, looking first at me and then Daniel through half-shut eyes, and said, "I'll take it."

Visibly strained, Daniel tried to find a way to get his practiced sales pitch in. He was clearly debating whether he should check to see if his spontaneous shoppers had any idea of what the prices were. His anguish was brought to an end by a resolute colleague. She walked up to us, introduced herself as Mrs. Grönke, and telling us she had just attended a mattress seminar, began to impose the fruits of her wisdom. Still lying down and bobbing her hips up and down on the mattress, Luise was subjected to the detailed differences between latex, feather core, and tempur as Mrs. Grönke worked up to full speed. The sight of Luise bouncing away like a kid in the presence of the prim sales assistant threatened to make a fit of giggles take hold again, so I moved on a few meters.

While Luise worked her way steadfastly and earnestly through all of the possible sleeping positions, I stopped in front of a chest of drawers that would look wonderful in my hall—920 euros. The lamp on it emphasized the warm tone of the wood—320 euros. I liked it. I decided to buy both.

Half an hour later we were sitting opposite Daniel at a glass table. In front of us were two glasses of champagne. We wrote our addresses down again while Daniel wrote two separate receipts, reading each section out loud to us and watching us closely. We looked back without betraying any reaction.

Once our credit cards had been put through, we stood up slowly, Daniel looking relieved. I thanked him and shook his hand, which put him in a muddle again. Luise did the same, giving a beaming smile while she shook his hand and thanked him as emphatically as though he had just given us everything for free. Looking embarrassed, he immediately turned around and took two small white porcelain vases from a display dining table. With a grand gesture, he handed them to us.

"May I offer you ladies a little something, for two such charming customers."

We bowed appropriately and left the shop with control-led posture and without looking at each other. We walked through Stilwerk, collecting Luise's reserved purchases on the way. Determined and without exchanging a single word, we made our way to the parking lot. Just before getting to our cars, in the middle of the parking lot, we both stopped, looked at each other, and the suppressed laughter burst forth.

I held the little vase towards Luise. "May I offer you..."

Our laughter became hysterical. Luise held her sides. "He thought we couldn't pay." The tears were running down her face.

So were mine. "Luise, we just spent over eight thousand euros in just forty-five minutes."

She gasped for air and then carried on laughing loudly.

"And we didn't even try to barter."

I had a stitch. I looked at the vase. The laughter started to build up again.

"But we've got two vases which we can fit roughly two small flowers in."

We were crouched next to one another in the middle of the parking lot, elegant shopping bags all around us, our faces deep red, and laughing like two teenagers. Passersby looked at us in amazement. A few smiled. Eventually, we wiped our tears away and pulled ourselves together. Luise took deep and concentrated breaths in and out. "God, that was fun!" We walked slowly over to our cars. I felt both lighthearted and grown up at the same time. I'd never spent money with such abandon in my whole life.

Once we were standing in front of Luise's car, she looked at her watch and said, "So, what are we doing now?"

Charlotte whispered, *The ring, the jeweler in the Lange Reihe.*

I glanced briefly at my lonely hand. Before Edith could butt in I quickly said, "I'd like to show you a ring in a shop on the Lange Reihe that I really like. There was no price on it though. And then afterwards we can take our cars and bags home and then meet up later at Casa di Roma to have a meal and celebrate."

"Wonderful." Luise nodded. "Although, in your current state of mind I don't think the price will be an issue."

Charlotte smiled. I didn't let Edith get a word in edgewise.

By the end of this amazing day we were sitting in our favorite Italian restaurant with two glasses of Taittinger Rose in front of us.

"If we're doing it, we've got to do it right."

Luise hadn't hesitated in ordering the most expensive champagne on the menu. I turned my hand so that the small stone in my white gold ring sparkled in the candlelight.

"One thousand six hundred and thirty euros," was the jeweler's answer when I asked after the price.

Without hesitating, Charlotte had said, *Much more beautiful than your stupid wedding ring.*

And Luise had leaned over to me and whispered, "Go on, try it on, and if it fits, take it."

It fit. Of course it did.

Edith was outnumbered. And now my hand looked beautiful and confident.

Luise followed my gaze and said happily, "You've done it. The first half year, your new life, and you've replaced your wedding ring. You know, seeing you gives me strength. To us, and to life."

We clinked our glasses together. Before we drank, another thought came to my mind.

"Do you know what? I've spent seven thousand six hundred and ninety euros today. And with relish. Next I'll pay back Georg the five thousand euros he lent me, which will be a relief. Then there'll still be exactly two thousand three hundred and ten left over from Bernd's fifteen thousand. That's not much. We'll spend at least a hundred euros tonight; well, let's say a hundred and ten, so that'll leave two thousand two hundred. And the only man I have to confess not having saved more of it to is my tax consultant. And however much he shakes his head, at the end of the day he still gets paid by me, and so he won't say anything really. Luise, I feel like I've made it."

Contentedly, we nodded at one another.

Richard

Dorothea spread her arms out wide and fell back into my red dream chair, swinging her legs up onto the footstool. She looked first at the ceiling and then at me.

"Wonderful. You did good! How much did this darling cost then?"

I looked at her. Black suede suit, expensive black shoes—and the red of her lipstick matched the chair perfectly.

"Two thousand two hundred euros."

Dorothea stroked the chair arm slowly. "That's fine, just buy four less pairs of shoes."

I laughed. Dorothea's view of the world—in terms of shoes at least—was very different from mine. "Dorothea, that's at least twenty pairs."

She looked critically at my sneakers and sighed. "That's exactly your problem. You'd get at least twenty pairs of those for that, yes, but I'm talking about real shoes." She stretched out her leg and made small circles with her foot. "Shoe culture, sweetheart, Manolo Blahnik."

I looked skeptically at the soft leather, the pointed toe, and high heel.

"I could never walk in shoes like that."

Dorothea circled both feet, looking at them as though she were in love.

"Beautiful shoes aren't supposed to be comfortable; they're supposed to give you attitude." She stood up.

"Someday I'll get you to buy your first pair of Prada mules; then you'll understand."

After she'd examined and enthused about the rest of my purchases, we settled down in the lounge and opened a bottle of champagne. We'd hardly seen each other over the last few weeks, just spoken on the phone now and then. Dorothea had had one television production after another, and my schedule had been packed lately as well. I updated her on the recent events, my appointment with Rüdiger, and on Luise's apartment and her move last week.

Dorothea looked sympathetic. "How did moving out go? Have you seen her?"

"She had a moving company do it all. Dirk stayed with friends for the weekend, so she was alone to do the packing in the morning. I went over to see her at the new place at midday, and she wasn't doing too good. She was feeling awful about Dirk, she's never really lived alone before, and for some reason she still hasn't heard from Alex. It's all pretty terrible."

Dorothea poured herself some champagne and said, "Moving out is always miserable. When I moved out of Georg's, I had a fever and the shivers for three days."

I could still remember it. "And you two hadn't even separated at that point. You just didn't want to live together anymore; the break-up came a year later."

Dorothea shook her head and laughed a little. "What does 'want to' mean? We only managed to live together for three months, after a five-year relationship. He was ruled by his head and I by my heart, and we had two completely different body clocks and routines. I paint at night, Georg gets up early; I'm hungry in the evening, Georg at midday; I don't like talking in the morning, Georg is tired in the evenings; he's tidy, I'm creative. We had to make so many compromises that there wouldn't have been anything of ourselves left over. If we'd carried on, we wouldn't have recognized each other. I can only handle love with physical distance, that's what I've learned."

I thought about myself, about my lack of enthusiasm for cooking and shopping for myself, about cold beds and dark apartments, about double-locked front doors that need two turns of the key when you get home.

"Don't you miss having someone to look after, who looks after you and is waiting at home for you sometimes?"

Dorothea looked at me, amazed. "Why would I? I look after myself, and I do it better than anyone else. When I come home I don't want to talk right away, so I'm happy that I don't have to. And I like the fact that my apartment looks exactly the same in the evenings as it did when I left it that morning. I can have a grouchy face, lie around in bed all day, I can eat whenever and whatever I want, speak on the phone when and for as long as I like, and lie in the bath for three hours. I think it's great."

"And you never feel lonely?"

Dorothea thought for a moment. "You know, the company I most enjoy is my own. So if I get hormonal urges now and then, I call Nils. But that's not something I want every day."

Nils was a musician, lived in Cologne, and was married. Dorothea had met him three years ago at a filming. She rarely spoke about him; he popped up now and again, stayed a few days, and then was gone again for weeks on end. Dorothea seemed content with this state of affairs; she regarded as him as her private pleasure and declined any explanations.

"I'm not suited to being part of a couple. I tried with Georg, but it didn't work. And I just don't enjoy it long-term."

I thought about Nina. She was the other extreme. Dorothea hadn't met her yet, but I told her about our get-togethers, the conversation about single life, and her search for a new man.

Dorothea listened with a look of disbelief.

"Honey, that sounds awful. Togetherness at any price, as long as it looks good from the outside and you're not living alone. I can't understand why forty-something women can't be happy with themselves. As if some guy is a guarantee of a better life." Then she looked at me, startled. "Christine, I didn't mean you."

I'd become lost in thought and had stood up to make some cappuccinos with the new espresso machine. "You're right though. All I had in the last five years with Bernd was a façade. I felt neither loved nor desired, but I thought everything else would have been even worse."

I went into the kitchen. Dorothea called after me. "By the way, do you still remember Richard?"

I flinched. Charlotte sighed.

I turned the machine on. Without turning away from the chrome masterpiece, I called out in answer to Dorothea's question.

"Richard. Oh yes, what makes you mention him?"

"No need to shout at me." Dorothea was standing in the kitchen door.

I pressed the wrong button and hot water spritzed next to the milk jug.

Dorothea shoved a cup underneath it. She laughed. "You have to be on the ball with these high-tech machines, you know. What's up? Two glasses of champagne and you're already all over the place?"

I looked at her while I wiped away the water. "I have no idea. Perhaps I can't handle champagne during the day anymore." I carried on wiping until Dorothea took the cloth from my hand. In the end, I asked anyway.

"What about Richard?"

Dorothea threw the cloth in the sink and looked at me questioningly.

"Richard? Oh yes, I ran into him last weekend. I was in Bremen for Anneke's fiftieth birthday—you remember, the mask artist. You met her at my birthday—the tall, beautiful redhead. She's divorced too now, by the way."

I took a deep breath.

"Yes, I remember. And?"

"Nothing really. It was a great birthday party. And Richard was there too; they knew each other from Berlin. How did I get onto that?"

She thought for a moment, biting her lower lip.

"Oh, I know, the thing about façades. Richard had a lot of problems in his private life in Berlin for a long while—at least that's what Georg told me. Demanding wife, massive arguments, and he just put up with it all. That's what Georg said. In any case, he handed in his notice at the station—he was a lawyer for years, if you remember—and is now living in Bremen where he runs a media law practice with a colleague, and he seems to be very successful."

Edith piped up while I was still taking in what I'd heard. *It was six years ago; he won't even remember you.*

Dorothea continued. "I was supposed to say hi to you from him; I completely forgot about that. I'd forgotten that you knew each other. Well, in any case, as I was saying, he seems to have put all those personal issues behind him and is living in Bremen. Hang on a moment, he gave me his card."

She went out to the hallway, fetched her bag from the new chest of drawers, and emptied it out.

Charlotte whispered excitedly. *Richard. And now of all times!*

Dorothea came back and triumphantly pressed a crumpled card into my hand. "Come on, nothing gets past me. Give him a call. He's a nice guy, and you're in Bremen quite a bit." She looked at the clock. "Oh hell, is that the time? I was supposed to be at the TV station twenty minutes ago." Hectically, she packed all her things back into her handbag, blew me a kiss, and disappeared through the door, which clicked shut loudly behind her.

I sat down slowly at the kitchen table and stared at the card.

I read the name again and again, the address of his office, his private address. He still had the same mobile number. My heartbeat was quickening, and it felt as though

I couldn't get enough air. Decisively, I stood up, grabbed my jacket and bag, and left the apartment, planning to walk around the Alster Lake at least once.

Half an hour later I slowed my pace and let the memories flood back.

It was six years ago.

Georg and Dorothea were working for a television channel based in Berlin. Georg still lived there back then. After their unsuccessful attempt at living together, Dorothea had moved back to Hamburg. Once a year the station hosted a summer party. Dorothea could never understand my fascination with the world of TV back then.

"Stick to the book trade," she'd said. "These TV types have all got a screw loose."

I refused to believe her, so to "cure" me she sent Bernd and I an invitation to the summer party. I was excited—a whole weekend in Berlin, and with a summer party and TV people too. And perhaps it would do Bernd and I good; our relationship was going through some changes back then. It would be the first time in months that we would have a chance to get away from the countryside and the daily grind together.

Bernd only gave the invitation a quick glance.

"I'm not going to Berlin just for one evening. That's ridiculous."

I tried to convince him.

"But we could spend the weekend there and look around Berlin. And I'm sure the party will be fun. We can stay at Georg's, so it won't cost anything."

Bernd wouldn't give in. "I want to go sailing with Adrian on Sunday. And besides, I don't know anyone there."

I was disappointed. "I don't know anyone there either, apart from Georg and Dorothea. But that doesn't matter; maybe we'll meet some nice people. Come on, we don't do anything together anymore."

But Bernd was done discussing it. "I've got neither the time nor the inclination, and that's the end of it. Go there by yourself if you really want to."

I told Georg and Dorothea that Bernd had to work and went there alone by train. They picked me up from the station in the early afternoon and took me to their favorite haunts around Berlin. We went all over the city. I was enraptured with the big city atmosphere, and I found myself missing the Bernd I used to know.

The summer party was that evening. I had bought myself a red dress, was full of anticipation, and wanted to love every second of it. Dorothea noted my excitement somewhat sympathetically and murmured lightly, "Don't get too worked up or you'll just be disappointed."

Two hours later I understood her skepticism.

The majority of the almost eight hundred guests were very young, very blond media yuppies who were almost all dressed in black. They were in their mid twenties at the most, had identical outfits, which looked like uniforms, shrill voices, and very little to say. I wasn't up to scratch in the small talk, and I felt old and inappropriately dressed.

George noticed my anguished expression and pulled me towards a small bar nearby. We collapsed onto two leather chairs and both sighed deeply. The loud music was muffled here, and the air was better than in the other rooms.

My brother looked at me and laughed. "I told you they were mostly all media lemmings and big cheeses. But… there are exceptions."

I suddenly felt someone was standing behind me. I heard a deep voice that made my stomach feel strange.

"And here comes the exception. Hi, Georg."

Georg stood up, looking pleased, and held out his hand to a tall, dark-haired man. "Richard, it's great that you could make it. I thought you were on vacation."

Richard smiled, looking first at me, then Georg, whose hand he was shaking. "It gets worse every year at this party. And younger."

I reckoned he was about forty.

His gaze turned back to me. I stared back, not moving, and felt as though I were glued to my seat. Georg took over the introductions. "Christine, this is Richard Jürgensen, our lawyer. Richard, this is my sister Christine who, until today, was a big TV fan, but who's now probably going to return ruefully to her books."

Richard's hand was warm; he clasped mine tightly. His eyes were very blue.

"Very pleased to meet you."

I had the feeling he actually meant the well-worn phrase.

Meanwhile, I'd circled around half of the Alster. There was a vacant bench right down by the dock. I sat down, watched two nearby swans, and lit myself a cigarette. My thoughts wandered back to that night again.

Nothing spectacular had happened at the party. We stayed sitting in the small bar. Richard pulled a chair up alongside mine and stayed by my side. In the course of the evening more and more of Georg and Richard's colleagues joined us, and so our circle of refugees from the main party grew steadily.

Richard, with his charm and humor, was the center of attention. Not that he tried to be. He was certainly the center of *my* attention. I sat there, listened to him, laughed at his stories, was amazed at his quick-wittedness, and was touched by his careful manners.

And I fell in love. That's all.

The next morning Dorothea, Georg, and I went out for brunch together. I wasn't in the mood for talking and was still back in that small bar in my thoughts, thinking of the feeling I'd had when my knee had brushed against Richard's leg. Almost accidentally.

Georg and Dorothea put my silence down to too much alcohol and gossiped about the partygoers. They said very little about Richard, and I didn't trust myself to ask. Georg only mentioned that he was a great guy, but unfortunately with a tendency for having a difficult private life. "I don't really know much about it. He doesn't talk about it much. But he's on his second marriage, and he has two children from the first whom he rarely sees. And his current wife is apparently a rather complicated person. I've never met her; she doesn't come to the station or to parties. She doesn't seem particularly interested in his work."

Dorothea knew a lawyer from his department.

"Susanne told me that Richard's wife is horrendous; they met her somewhere once. An arrogant cow apparently."

Georg gave Dorothea a reproachful look.

"You don't even know her. Susanne may have met her briefly, but that doesn't mean anything. You're all so quick to judge."

Dorothea nodded at him smugly. "You're such a saint."

Georg looked thoughtful.

"But I don't reckon he's happy either. The poor guy. And he deserves to be."

Later, when I sat on the train, on my way home and to Bernd, I thought about why I hadn't told Georg or Dorothea about the feelings Richard had provoked in me.

Edith knew the answer: *Because it's ridiculous. He's married, you're married, it was just the atmosphere of the summer party. You were never even alone with him. You don't know him at all.*

Charlotte was in love. *He sat next to you the whole evening. And the looks he gave you. He felt good in your company.*

Edith groaned loudly. *He sat there because it was the only free chair. Good grief, he'll have forgotten you already. Wake up—you're thirty-four, not thirteen.*

Bernd picked me up from the station. He seemed pleased that I was back. We went to the Chinese restaurant on the way home. During the meal I told Bernd about the party. When I mentioned the name Richard Jürgensen, my heart started to pound. Bernd seemed to notice something and asked a question for the first time during my account of the partygoers.

"Richard Jürgensen. Do I know him from TV?"

"No, he's a lawyer for the station."

Bernd piled rice onto his plate.

"Oh, okay. I thought he was someone special."

Over the next weeks and months, I dreamed of Richard now and then and thought about the feeling I'd had in his presence. After a while, the details of his face faded, but a feeling of longing remained. I made an effort not to let the thoughts in.

After all, I had Bernd.

Half a year later we received the next invitation. In Berlin again, and again on a Saturday. This time Georg was one of the three guests of honor at a joint birthday party. The date was in three weeks' time. That evening Georg phoned.

"I know it's a bit short notice, but it was a spur-of-the-moment idea. Can you guys make it?"

This time Bernd really couldn't; he had to go to a trade fair in Munich.

"I'll come by myself again. Bernd's fair has been arranged for ages. I can come with Ines."

"It's a shame that Bernd can't make it. Oh well, never mind. Anyway, Christine, would you mind sleeping in a hotel? I can't manage to put everyone up at my place."

"Sure, that's no problem."

"Great. Ines is staying with a friend of hers, so you can arrange to travel up together between yourselves."

I thought briefly of Richard, and I wanted to ask Georg whether he was invited. Bernd came into the room and said, "Give him my best, and tell him to pop by sometime." I swallowed the question about Richard and, afterwards, was happy I'd done so.

Three weeks later Ines and I climbed out of a taxi in front of a trendy bar in Berlin. We were a little late; the route from my hotel to Gundula's apartment had been a little longer than I thought. My hotel was near the bar, so really Ines should have picked me up and not the other way around, but neither of us had thought of that.

Ines laughed as I paid the bill.

"That's what happens when you don't check the map. You insisted on picking me up, so I just assumed you knew the area."

I kept the receipt, asking myself why at the same time, and said, "I'm the oldest. It's my responsibility. Come on."

The bar was full, the music not too loud, the buffet Italian. We made our way through the guests, looking for Georg. We waved to a few familiar faces, some of Georg's old friends from college and elsewhere. Dorothea was standing behind the bar, gesticulating wildly, pointing to her left and blowing us kisses. We followed her lead and pushed our way up to Georg.

"Happy birthday, big brother."

Ines hugged him.

"Christine has our present. This is a great bar."

I kissed Georg on the cheek, gave him a big hug, and pushed a Manufactum voucher for store credit into his jacket pocket. He felt the envelope and beamed.

"Thank you, what a surprise!"

Georg hated birthday presents, and even as a child he'd suffered from extreme anxiety about getting presents he couldn't bring himself to act pleased about. That's why we'd been giving him a voucher for his favorite shop for years. Only the sum varied.

He looked around.

"I think you already know a lot of the people here; as you can see, I won't be able to look after you that much."

"Don't worry."

I watched Ines, who had discovered Malte with a cry of joy. Georg followed my gaze.

"Look, Malte and Ines. When she was six, she wanted to have his babies."

A new group of guests arrived. Georg turned to greet them, and I made my way to the bar. On the way I looked at all the faces, suddenly realizing who I was looking for. I couldn't see him, and I sensed my disappointment. Dorothea had fought her way through to me and held a cocktail in front of my nose.

"Sex on the Beach. I know you love it."

She giggled. I tried it. "If your jokes were as good as your cocktails, life would be a lot more fun. It tastes great. Cheers."

Dorothea laughed anyway. "I think my jokes are superb. Oh, I've got to go back to the bar. See you in a bit." I drank and watched her go.

As I felt his hand on my shoulder, I almost choked on my drink.

"I was hoping you'd be here."

That voice, those blue eyes. And he still had his hand on my shoulder. If we were in a comic strip, a sea of flowers would have exploded around my head. In real life, my pulse was racing. My brain tried to come up with hundreds of intelligent and witty lines.

I said, "Oh, hello, Richard." And then spilled my orange-red cocktail all over my white trousers.

Six years later, sitting on the bench on the Alster, I had to smile at the memory. I stood up, stubbed out my cigarette in a paper towel, and walked slowly on. I hadn't taken in much more of the party, although I'm sure it was a great one. Richard was all I could remember. He had come alone. We stayed together the whole evening, first standing with the other party guests, and then we sat down by ourselves in a corner. We drank a bottle of red wine together, and smoked and talked. I don't know which of us started. Or about what. We talked about his job, about mine, about brothers and sisters, about books, about TV.

The air became sticky, the music louder. We looked at each other briefly and then stood up. Our search for a more peaceful location proved to be unsuccessful. Richard bent over to me to whisper, and his mouth brushed my ear. I got goose bumps.

He asked, "Shall we go for a walk? I'd like to get out of here."

Instead of answering, I stroked my hand over his back, which shocked even me. He took my hand in his and pulled me towards the exit.

We walked through the dark streets and talked about our lives. I can't remember what came over us; we were barely stoppable. His first marriage, the horrendous divorce, which was mostly about money and carried out at the expense of the children. Then about my marriage and how it had developed into a house share, the fact that I hadn't had children, and about the desires I had that couldn't be fulfilled by Bernd because he didn't even know them. His second wife, who had been the reason for his divorce, and who had obviously had a very different idea of who he was.

"You know, I think all she wanted was to get me for herself. Once she'd achieved her goal, she moved on to her first affair. A year after we got married."

"My husband hasn't wanted to sleep with me for the last two years. Perhaps that's what marriage is like."

We went to sit in a bar for a while and sat in silence while we warmed up. Richard took my hand and held it between his. "A strange night. Nothing like this has ever happened to me."

I looked at him for a long while. I felt like I wanted to burn the image of his face into my mind.

"Nor me. It's confusing."

We left the bar and walked slowly on. I knew the way to the hotel; in another life I'd come along here in a taxi. I looked at myself. Richard had clasped his hand with mine and put them in his jacket pocket. I brushed my thumb over his warm skin. I could feel his presence with every pore, and I thought about my familiar life, about Bernd, about Richard's wife. Everything was circling around in my head. He was silent.

Then we were standing in front of my hotel. I didn't know what to think.

I heard Charlotte. *Ask him if he's coming up. Go on.*

And Edith. *It'll just be complicated. It would turn your whole life upside down. This man will get under your skin. You won't be able to handle it.*

Richard kissed me softly on the lips. He looked at me sadly.

"I would love to sleep with you. But I'd end up hurting you too. I've got a lot of things to sort out in my life, and I haven't even made a start yet. Perhaps tonight has released something in me that will finally give me the courage to make some changes. But it's going to be a long journey. And I like you too much to ask that of you."

I realized that my eyes were filling with tears. I couldn't say anything, just touched his cheek gently. He was still looking at me.

"Thank you, Christine. This was the best night I've had in a very long time. Especially because it's ending like this and will stay something special."

Something occurred to me. I turned aside and looked in my handbag for the taxi receipt and a pen. My hands shaking, I ripped the receipt in half and wrote my mobile number on the first half. Richard took the other half, wrote his number, and put it back in my bag.

I tried to find my voice.

"Maybe we can talk on the phone sometime."

He smiled and brushed his finger over my lips. His voice was raw.

"Definitely. This was too good to just lose touch."

He walked off to the taxi line. I watched him go, feeling light, alive, and yet very sad.

Having made my way all around the Alster, I went back to my apartment. So much had happened since then. The week after that night in Berlin, Bernd had had a serious car crash. I found out at two a.m. when the police called me, telling me the name of the hospital but not how he was. I drove almost an hour to get there, full of panic and blinded by tears. I felt guilty, was scared of losing Bernd. I swore to myself that I would never allow myself to have the feelings and thoughts that I'd had with Richard again.

Bernd was very lucky; his injuries weren't life-threatening. I sat thankfully by his bed the whole night staring at his bruised face. In my thoughts I asked both Bernd and Richard for forgiveness.

I opened both locks on my apartment door and went in.

In the years that followed, I had dreamt of Richard now and again; he was still there somewhere, in my soul. We had only spoken on the telephone once; he had phoned me two days after the accident, and it was a short conversation. Both of us were in shock.

I still knew his mobile number by heart. I sat down in my red chair, poured the last of the champagne from Dorothea's glass, and drank it down. I looked around my apartment. A great deal had happened since that night, and Richard didn't know about any of it.

I heard Dorothea's voice in my ear.

"He said to say hi to you from him. He seems to have put all those personal issues behind him and is living in Bremen. Why don't you give him a call?"

I smoked two cigarettes, one after another, and thought for a while. Then I stood up and looked for the telephone.

Stage Fright

eonie stood up slowly, went over to the door of the sauna, and turned over the hourglass that was hanging next to it. Her gaze fell on a woman who was lying on her back on the lower bench, and then she sat back on her hand towel and gestured at me to join her on the lower level. I stood up and took my towel over, leaned over, and whispered, "What is it?"

She gestured towards the woman again. I looked, but she didn't seem familiar to me at all. I looked back at Leonie questioningly and shrugged my shoulders.

She shook her head and whispered, "In a moment."

I leaned back and watched the hourglass. The minutes trickled untiringly down in the sand. I was slowly starting to sweat.

Leonie and I met every two weeks for a sauna day; it had now become a ritual of ours. Leonie's husband Michael had come along with us once. Over our post-sauna beers he had decided—feigning bewilderment—that he didn't want to accompany us there again. He felt himself to be too manly and naïve to follow our girl talk without lasting damage. Of course, we didn't have the slightest clue what he was referring to.

The woman next to us sat up and stretched. Looking at the hourglass, she stood up, wrapped herself up in her towel, and left the sauna. Now we were alone. As soon as the door had swung shut, Leonie turned to me.

"There's no way they were real."

I was still trying to work out if the woman looked familiar to me, and I had no idea what Leonie meant. "What weren't real?"

Leonie looked at me indignantly. "My God, Christine, are you blind? Her breasts were fake. And not particularly good ones at that. You could tell right away!"

"I can't believe the things you look at. Michael would have been horrified."

"My darling husband would have noticed too. Those things practically poke you in the eye."

Leonie had to laugh at what she'd just said.

The sweat was running down my face. I looked at the hourglass; we'd been in there for twenty minutes now. I stood up. "That's enough for me. I'm done."

A little later we lay wrapped in bathrobes and blankets on two teak loungers on the covered roof terrace. Leonie looked up at the glorious blue sky.

"It still looks like summer, but it smells like fall."

I turned my head towards her. "It's September—the summer's nearly over."

Leonie turned on her side, propped her head up on her bent arm, and looked at me. "Do you have the fall blues?"

"What makes you say that? It was you who brought it up."

She looked at me thoughtfully.

"I don't know. You're so quiet today. Is something wrong?"

I shook my head.

Charlotte nodded. *Richard.*

Edith answered. *Oh great, now it's getting you in such a state that everyone's noticing. Excellent.*

Leonie was still watching me. When I didn't answer, she turned back over onto her back. Her voice sounded a little peeved.

"You don't have to tell me if you don't want to. But you were so curt on the phone the night before last. I was just asking."

She stared into the distance. I gave the arm of her bathrobe a placatory tug.

"If there was something wrong, I would tell you about it. It was just that I was waiting for another call the other evening. That's why I was a little short."

I paused, but Leonie didn't ask. But she did turn her head and look at me again. "So I'm supposed to believe that there's nothing bothering you at the moment? I know you, Christine. There's something on your mind."

I tried to think of something to say that would neither be a lie nor give too much away.

"It's nothing I can really explain. It's just that I've got too much time on my hands at the moment; almost all of my appointments are done, and I only have a handful of visits left to make. When I have that much free time, so many thoughts go through my head. Like whether I'll manage to get to grips with living alone, whether I can ever fall in love again, whether I even want to get into another relationship, whether I can ever trust anyone again, things like that."

I felt that I'd sailed smoothly around the topic of Richard. Leonie sat up.

"Of course you'll fall in love again. And once you've done that, you'll be able to get involved again. It just needs time. First just find yourself a lover, no strings, just to feel some intimacy. After all, you need sex now and again too."

I stared at her, amazed.

"Leonie, you're not seriously telling me to become someone's lover?"

She had stood up now and was looking down at me.

"Gosh, don't be such a prude! I'm not saying you should start having an affair right away, but it's okay to be aware of your needs and to want to have them fulfilled. You're going to be forty in eight weeks; don't be so inhibited."

I was speechless. Leonie noticed and laughed. She sat on the foot of my lounger and laid her hand on my covered legs.

"Look at it like this. There are two possibilities. Either you have a partner who knows your needs, takes them seriously, and does his best to fulfill them. If you have that, you're lucky. Or, you have a partner who doesn't really care about your needs and doesn't consider himself responsible for meeting them, and then you might as well forget it. Unfortunately, you had the second with Bernd, but don't make the mistake of suppressing your needs again—you have a right to them."

She stood up again and looked at the time.

I couldn't stop myself from asking. "Which one is it for you?"

Leonie smiled. "I'm very lucky. But now, I have an appointment with my lovely masseur. That's one of the few needs that Michael can't fulfill. So for the last two years he's been giving me vouchers for ten massage sessions as a birthday present. So, off I go. See you later."

I watched as she disappeared through the glass door into the spa. I wrapped my cold feet up snugly in the woolen blanket and lay back comfortably. Leonie's words stayed in my mind. My needs really had fallen by the wayside in recent years, and to be honest I wasn't even sure what they were anymore.

Charlotte knew one. *Richard is a need.*

The thought of having Richard as my lover made my heart start to pound.

Edith was against it. *Nonsense, you're being dumb again— you'll just fall in love immediately. And then you can forget it.*

I burrowed deeper into my bathrobe. I had that "Richard" feeling in my stomach again.

On that evening two weeks ago I'd picked the phone up at least twenty times, and I put it down again just as many. I painted my toenails, cleaned the bathroom mirror, filed all of my bank statements, ironed three blouses, and then opened a bottle of red wine. I thought about it for the duration of the first glass, and then at nine p.m., I phoned Richard. As I dialed the code for Bremen, I felt my pulse start to race.

He answered after the second ring.

"Jürgensen."

My mind felt empty, my mouth dry. I sought desperately for an opening line. Richard was impatient, had no idea of my torment.

"Hello, who's there?"

I hurried to speak and took the plunge.

"Hello, Richard, um, it's Christine, me, I mean…
Georg's sister."

Edith rolled her eyes. *Great opener.*

At the other end there was a small pause. Then he
found his voice again. It sounded guarded.

"Christine. How nice to hear from you. How are you?"

I hadn't been able to imagine what his reaction would
be; I wasn't expecting shouts of joy or tears, but this "nice"
sounded so wrong. I tried to sound casual.

"I'm good thanks. Dorothea mentioned that you'd
passed on your best and she gave me your card, so I thought
I'd give you a call. Just to see how you're doing."

Edith shook her head. *What a stupid thing to say.*

Richard didn't seem to have expected anything else.
His answer sounded noncommittal.

"Oh yes, Anneke's birthday. Dorothea told me that
you were still in contact even though she's not with your
brother anymore. That's really great. How is Georg, anyway? I haven't heard from him in ages. Is he still in Berlin?"

This was going all wrong. So different from the conversation I'd had in my mind while I was walking mawkishly
around the Alster.

Edith again. *I told you.*

Charlotte was still hopeful.

I answered Richard's question.

"No, Georg is living in Hamburg too now. He's been
there for two years. He's a freelance journalist and has lots
of commissions. He's doing well."

Pause.

Then Richard again.

"Aha. That's great. What do you mean, he lives there too? Oh yes, your sister lives there, right? What's her name again, Iris?"

"Ines."

"Yes, that's right. That's great. So you've got two places you can stay at in Hamburg now."

Edith was going crazy. *This is just getting worse and worse.*

I lit up a cigarette and noticed that my hand was shaking.

Richard picked up on it. "You still smoke."

For the first time I could hear a smile in his voice. I cleared my throat.

"Yes, I still smoke. And I don't need places to stay in Hamburg anymore. I live here now."

Pause.

Then his voice, neutral again. "Had you two had enough of country life?"

"Not us, me."

Now I was curious.

His answer was disappointing. "Oh right, well, I did it the other way around. I've moved out of Berlin into a Bremen suburb—well, almost a village, really. But you get used to it."

Charlotte begged. *Go on, ask him something personal.*

Edith stopped. *This is probably the dumbest phone conversation you've had in years.*

Agreeing with her, I sat up straight.

"Anyway, Richard, I didn't mean to disturb you. I was just calling because of Dorothea and the card. So, I hope you have a lovely evening."

Richard's answer was just as noncommittal.

"Sure, thanks for calling. Maybe we could have lunch sometime. I'm often in Hamburg on business."

Edith was off again. *"Lunch. It doesn't get much more businesslike than that. He'll probably claim it on his expenses."*

In desperation, I tried to sound casual.

"Sure, give me a call sometime. Have a nice evening."

Charlotte was absolutely miserable.

And Edith said, *The ass didn't even ask for your phone number.*

I stayed sitting in my upright posture at the table, the phone still clasped in my hand, and felt the intense desire to throw it across the room and against the wall. Instead, I stood up and quickly paced twice around my apartment to calm myself down. When I came to a standstill, I was in front of my red sanctuary of an armchair. I let myself fall into it, then stood up, angrily fetched my wine glass, and sank back down again.

Edith was rubbing salt into the wound. *You're making a fool of yourself, having these crazy daydreams all day long, expecting God knows what from some guy that you haven't heard from in six years—and then you're disappointed when he brushes you off. You're so sensitive!*

Charlotte was still bewildered. *But there was something between you in Berlin. You didn't just make it up. And he was the one that told Dorothea to say hello to you, so maybe he was just a bit overwhelmed and startled by your call.*

Edith laughed mockingly. *Overwhelmed! Ha! That must be a joke. We're talking about an evening that took place six years ago. It's been forgotten. You're acting like you're thirteen again. You were just the same with David Cassidy when you had his*

Bravo *poster above your bed. But that was thirty years ago. Don't be so childish.*

I was annoyed when I felt the tears. It really was childish. I'd gotten swept up in the memory. Perhaps Nina's longing had been infectious and I was mutating into one of these single women who are consumed by their search for love.

"I won't let that happen. Not after everything I've achieved."

I realized that I'd just said the last sentence out loud. If I told Dorothea that I was starting to talk out loud to myself, she would rush me into one of her favorite shoe shops that very same day. She solved all small problems by buying new shoes.

And this was only a small problem—not even a problem really, just confusion.

Realizing that the wine was starting to go to my head, I went into the kitchen, poured the small amount that was left down the sink, and went to brush my teeth. Upstairs in bed I started to read my crime novel, but after three pages in which both the detective and the suspect had Richard's face, I turned the light out, my nerves shot.

In my dream, I was standing in front of a huge mountain of shoes and trying desperately to find a matching pair. I had a black heeled shoe in one hand, and in the other I only ever had brown or green or a different style. Dorothea stood next to me, smiling and putting pair after pair together. It was like a memory game; every time she matched a pair a bell rang.

I woke up as the ringing got louder and louder, and I reached sleepily for the light switch. Once I managed to decipher the time on the alarm clock, I realized I'd only been asleep for two hours. It was shortly before midnight and some idiot was phoning me at this time of night. I sat up, not wanting to go at first, but then images of accidents and other catastrophes came into my head. I sprang up, got the phone from the lounge table, and answered hoarsely.

I recognized his voice immediately; it sounded completely different now, almost urgent.

"Christine?"

In a shot, I was awake.

"Richard?"

Only then did our conversation come back to my mind.

"How did you get my number?"

Richard laughed quietly.

"I wrote it down from the display earlier. Christine, I reacted like an idiot. Can we forget the conversation we had earlier and start again?"

My heart pounded as I sank slowly into the red chair.

"I'd like that."

"I had quite a bad day today, and that's not supposed to be an excuse, but an explanation perhaps. Anyway, I was sitting in my apartment earlier, in a bad mood, and then when the telephone rang I thought it would just be more hassle. And when I heard your voice I was so pleased that I couldn't get a hold of myself quick enough. I'm sorry."

"Oh well, I wasn't exactly the epitome of wit either. It's just that you seemed so abrupt, and I wasn't expecting that."

Richard answered quickly. "I really didn't want to be like that, completely the opposite in fact. I was just unsure, you know? You're worked up, you want to be completely charming and say witty things, but then you just listen to yourself while you botch up the whole conversation."

"I know exactly what you mean."

I started to tremble, but I wasn't sure if I was nervous or cold. Richard heard it in my voice and said, "You were sleeping, weren't you? Are you still in the mood to chat?"

I was. I fetched my woolen blanket and cigarettes and snuggled up in the red chair with them.

And suddenly, the conversation just flowed. We picked up where we'd left off in Berlin six years ago. I told Richard about the last few months, beginning with the phone call from Bernd and ending with the red chair. He asked questions, and I answered. He started sentences, and I ended them. I asked him how he was, and he told me about the fights with Sabine, his second wife, about their arguments, power struggles, reconciliations, and resignations. Richard's marriage was becoming more and more of a façade, and he was becoming more and more indifferent to it. On top of that was his lack of interest in continuing to work as a lawyer for the TV station in Berlin.

"And then two years ago I met up with an old colleague from my studies. He had taken over a law practice in Bremen, wanted to specialize in media law and was looking for a partner. I thought it was a great idea. Sabine didn't waste any time in saying she didn't want to move to Bremen, so she stayed in Berlin, and I moved into a small apartment in Schwachhausen. I've got a great job and some peace and quiet during the week. It's better like this."

We spoke for over two hours. When I went to bed afterwards, my soul felt caressed.

Leonie was shaking my lounger. I opened my eyes and saw her looking down at me.

"Oh, Christine, that was really good. What's up? Were you asleep? You look like you were in another world."

I nodded briefly, stretched, and said, "Yes, I was just gone for a moment. Shall we go back to the sauna again?"

Leonie already had her towel over her arm. "Yes, right away. Come on, get that tired body of yours up."

The sauna was full this time, so we couldn't chat. Leonie discreetly observed the others in there and then shut her eyes.

I let my thoughts wander back to Richard.

After our first conversation we had spoken on the phone eight times over the last two weeks. Each conversation lasted at least an hour. I was surprised at how many things we found to talk about. Richard asked me all about my job, told me about his, and found it all fascinating. I told him about my booksellers and colleagues; he explained the basics of media law to me and described the cases he was working on.

We talked about books. He was a keen reader and let me recommend some to him, asking which Bremen bookstore he should get one of them from. Three days later he proudly told me the plot; he had read all through the night.

I felt like I'd known him for years, and the desire to meet up with him became stronger and stronger.

Charlotte was overjoyed; Edith kept silent. My anticipation for our phone conversations got me through the days.

We didn't talk about Sabine. I didn't dare to ask whether he went back to Berlin every weekend and still carried on with his marriage in spite of everything. He talked about the difficult years that had gone by, but never about what was happening now.

I suppressed my questions and thoughts and decided just to let things take their course.

Leonie sat up and switched seats. I sat down next to her. She smiled at me and then looked down at her red painted toenails. I felt a twinge of guilt for not telling her about Richard. She would have been happy, just for the fact that I was thinking about a man again. But I wasn't even sure what was going on yet. She looked at the hourglass and gestured with her head towards the door. We nodded to each other and went out to take a cold shower. Leonie didn't pick up on our conversation from before her massage again. We kept to more general topics; the sauna was full by now, and we were never alone.

After our second sauna trip, we had our usual post-sauna beers in the small bistro near the changing rooms. Leonie looked relaxed and content. She raised her glass.

"Just like being on vacation. That was great. Where are you off to tomorrow?"

I tried to keep my facial expression neutral. "I'm going to Bremen. I've got four appointments."

Leonie took a sip and wiped the foam from her mouth.

"That's fine. You'll be home early then."

"Yes," I said. And I thought, *Sorry, Leonie, but it's only a little white lie.*

That evening I packed my paperwork together and took my small travel bag from the cupboard. As I looked through my clothes and tried to decide what to wear, my excitement grew more and more. I sat on the bed and looked at the empty bag.

In our last phone conversation Richard had suddenly asked, "When will you next be in Bremen?"

"The day after tomorrow."

His answer came after a short pause.

"Then we should meet up."

Images jumped into my head. Berlin. His face. The kiss. The hotel. His apartment.

Edith piped up. *You've never stayed overnight in Bremen; that's ridiculous. You could be home within the hour.*

Charlotte answered. *You're going out for dinner with him, so see how you feel. You won't want to go home, for sure.*

Richard asked, "Shall I book you a hotel room? There's a hotel nearby that I sometimes put my clients up in. Then you can have a drink and you won't have to drive back to Hamburg at night."

I was relieved. "Thank you."

His voice betrayed a smile. "Great." He gave me the address.

"I'll pick you up from there at seven p.m., and then we'll have a lovely evening. Sound good?"

"Wonderful."

Which is exactly how I felt.

I looked for the new blouse that I'd bought with Dorothea in Eppendorf. She had convinced me to go for it; I'd thought the neckline was too low. Tonight though, it seemed fine, so I packed it. Along with my red lingerie.

Lying in my bed and pulling the image of Richard's face from my memory, I felt my stage fright. David Cassidy, I thought, and smiled.

Edith shook her head disapprovingly.

Charlotte whispered, *Tomorrow.*

I felt very happy.

Forty

t was Saturday evening, ten p.m. There had been a severe weather warning in the news; the fall storm that was sweeping over the north was supposed to get up to wind speeds of around 160 kilometers per hour.

It was the evening before my fortieth birthday.

I'd turned down Dorothea's suggestion of seeing the day in with a party, and I was instead sitting alone in my apartment, having pulled all the plugs from their sockets and lit two candles. With a mixture of fear and fascination, I watched the destruction the storm was causing outside my house.

On the table in front of me lay one of those women's magazines that are aimed at women over forty. I'd never had any interest in them; so far they'd had as little to do with me as those mind, body, and spirit or dog magazines. Yesterday Nina had brought a copy along to our squash game and had given it to me, laughing.

"Here, Christine, just so you know how you'll feel the day after tomorrow."

I was baffled, but thanked her politely and took the magazine.

Now, I leafed through the pages and still felt that it wasn't aimed at me. I wasn't planning on separating after twenty years of marriage, nor did I have problems with a pubescent daughter, nor was my boss twenty years younger than me. Menopause was another key topic, as well as facelifts, but none of it applied to me. I pushed the magazine aside and looked out of the window. A trash can slid past along the street.

Edith, however, wasn't done with the magazine.

In two hours you'll be forty, you **could** *have been married for twenty years, no plastic surgeon would rule out a facelift with you, and by the time your mother was forty you'd already finished your high school exams. You were already nineteen. You are* **exactly** *the target group for this magazine.*

A garden chair tipped over on my terrace. I stood up to see whether the wicker beach chair was holding up to the storm. It looked okay so far. The other chair spun over the paving stones.

I saw my reflection in the windowpane. Defiantly I smiled at myself and waited for Charlotte's voice. *You look good, not at all like a forty-year-old.*

Edith answered quickly. *Well, maybe not in this light.*

I sat back down at the table. My cell phone lay next to the wine glass and the ashtray. There were no notifications of text messages or calls on the display. I checked the reception; perhaps there were problems in the strong winds. But no, the network was stable. I pushed it aside and drew the wine glass nearer to me.

Forty.

I had got my qualifications, got myself a career, got married, and would soon be divorced. I would never be back at school, or become a professional sportswoman, nor have children. I didn't really belong to the target group of the trendier TV channels anymore, no one would say "young lady" to me, and the cosmetics industry had developed products for my mature skin.

I had done a lot of things right and just as many wrong. Tomorrow was my birthday. I sat here alone and felt increasingly downbeat.

The storm rattled the windows, and outside, my green plastic watering can flew by. I followed its path with my eyes; it was from my old life. My cell was still lying there quietly, not lighting up. I checked the display again. It was fine.

I stood up again and went to the patio door. The branches of the shrubs were dancing on the paving stones; the first branches whirled across the street. The cars were being driven along at a walking pace. My melancholy feeling got stronger, in keeping with the apocalyptic mood outside.

Forty.

Until this damn magazine I hadn't even thought about my age.

I was probably more than halfway through my life. And it was sure to have been the easier half. I started to feel uneasy.

Edith knew why. *No wonder, your life was always planned before. Bernd, the house, the job, your familiar circle of friends, everything and everyone getting old together. So there was no need to worry or be afraid. But now?*

Charlotte answered immediately. *Rubbish. You've got Hamburg, Luise, Dorothea, the red armchair, freedom, a new lease on life. And…*

Edith interrupted. *Don't say Richard. He's the real reason you're feeling sad. He won't be growing old with you; he's not even calling you. He's off with his wife, and you're turning forty all alone. Great.*

Charlotte tried to change the subject. *Dorothea offered to organize a party for you. Then there would have been lots of people here. But it's actually really nice to have a bit of peace and quiet.*

Edith didn't agree. *So what? Richard wouldn't be here either way. And that's what it's about right now.*

I surrendered and gave in to my thoughts. They wandered to Richard and the evening in Bremen two and a half months ago.

Richard had picked me up at the hotel. When I came into the foyer and saw him standing there, I felt like I'd been hit by lightning. I'd forgotten what it felt like to be near him and how blue his eyes were. I can't remember what we talked about in those first few minutes; it was like a silent film.

The Italian restaurant was only a few minutes from the hotel. It was pouring rain, so we ran closely alongside each other under Richard's umbrella. I loved the way he smelled.

At the restaurant we ordered, without conferring, the same dish and the same wine, and couldn't help but laugh. Once the wine was poured, Richard raised his glass, clinked it against mine, and said, with a thoughtful expression on his face, "To a wonderful evening. It's lovely that you're here."

He smiled. So did I.

I felt very at ease in his company. He was clever, charming, and very caring and witty. He told me about his law practice and his colleagues; I described the Bremen booksellers and my job. The conversation was easy; one topic led to the next. Now and again our knees touched under the table, and we pretended not to notice.

The second garden chair capitulated to the storm and flew into the hedge, which was swaying wildly in the wind. I stood back up and went over to the window with my glass of wine. The beach chair was still standing its ground.

We had drawn out the evening as much as we could, first ordering more wine, then coffee.

Once we were the last guests, Richard asked for the bill. We stood next to one another at the bar and drank a grappa on the house while we waited. I leaned my hip against his, and he looked at me and then put his arm around me. By the time we left the restaurant, the rain had stopped. We walked slowly back towards my hotel; Richard linked his arm with mine. Just before we got to the hotel, he stopped and looked at me solemnly.

"Christine, I've really enjoyed myself tonight. I would really love to go up to your room with you now, but there's something you should know."

He looked away for a moment, then back into my eyes.

"I've already told you a lot about my life. The thing is, it's been pretty stressful so far, and my marriage to Sabine is demanding too, but one horrendous divorce is enough for me. I know I don't want another one. It's something I feel you should know."

I answered him with a kiss, pulling him towards the entrance of the hotel.

Edith groaned loudly. *He told you the score, but of course you go and get swept up in the moment and let yourself in for all this nonsense anyway. You'll only have yourself to blame.*

My cell phone was still playing dead on the table. In ten minutes' time I would be forty.

Charlotte pushed some images into my mind. *Richard's face while he's asleep. Richard's face while he was making love to you. And it was nothing like the usual embarrassed first few times—when you're so aware that the other body is strange and unknown to you. It was intimate, easy, and wonderful. It was right.*

Edith reminded me. *What's right is that he left at four a.m. so none of his neighbors would notice that he wasn't home that night. And that's what he did the other times too.*

Charlotte answered. *He's just as smitten as you are. His feelings are genuine. Otherwise he wouldn't have phoned you the next day and told you that he wants to see you again.*

We'd met up every week since that night. Always on Wednesdays. To start with I'd rearranged my appointments, but since the tour had finished it was much easier. In the evenings we texted, and during the day we spoke on the phone. I was in love, and yet no one knew about it.

Edith was getting impatient. *And now you're in a state. On the weekend he's in Berlin, and you haven't heard from him since Thursday. You're waiting around for any sign of life from him and sitting in alone on your birthday.*

Midnight.

My cell beeped twice. A text message. I pressed the small envelope image and felt my heart rate quicken.

"All my love on your fortieth. Wishing you a new decade that even the gods would be jealous of. Georg."

I smiled, even though I could feel my disappointment trying to find its way out as tears. I went back to stand by the window with my glass. And crossed my fingers that Georg's wish would come true. One way or another.

My mobile beeped again. The second text.

"Birthday kiss. See you soon. Richard."

My soul felt calmed. That was a good start. I ignored Edith, gave Charlotte a wink, and went to bed, taking my phone with me.

Eight hours later I was awoken by the telephone ringing. My mother said hello as I sleepily answered.

"Good morning, birthday girl, we just wanted to wish you a wonderful day and to say we hope that all your dreams come true."

I was a little dizzy from getting up so quickly and had to lean against the kitchen table. I looked at the clock. Eight thirty a.m. I slowly pulled my thoughts together. My mother was on the phone, it was my birthday, I was now forty, and I needed coffee and a cigarette. But my mother wasn't done yet.

"Did you have one heck of a storm in Hamburg too? My goodness. I thought the roof was going to blow off, but everything's okay, we've checked. Why are you so sleepy still?"

"I woke up when the telephone rang. I don't set an alarm."

I looked at the espresso machine with longing. I couldn't use it while I was on the phone, it made too much noise. Mind you, so did my mother.

"Well, anyway, everything here is fine. And with you? You would have had to get up now anyway, wouldn't you? Or did you set the table last night?"

"Set the table?" I didn't understand what she meant. She seemed to notice and changed the subject.

"Okay darling, anyway, have a great day. I'll hand you over to your father now."

I continued to stare at the espresso machine. Then I heard my father's deep voice.

"Hello, Christine. I wish you good health, happiness, success, and for all your dreams to come true. How does it feel to be forty?"

I cleared my throat, but my voice still sounded croaky.

"Thank you. I feel just the same as always, really."

His answer sounded disapproving.

"You should really give up smoking, you know. I'm always reading about women over forty who smoke and have heart attacks."

I answered automatically. "Yes, if they're taking the pill, but I've weaned myself off of that."

He was flustered. Sometimes he could be a bit of a prude.

"Christine! Well, you're a grown-up. I only mean well. I don't want to interfere with your life. So, when are the guests arriving?"

I was still trying to figure out what guests he meant when I heard my mother's voice in the background.

"Oh, Rudi, you're not supposed to mention it—it's Ines's surprise!"

I stood up and turned the espresso machine on.

"Okay, daughter, you heard her. Forget what I said. So, happy birthday again and have a great day."

We said goodbye. I put the phone back and let the espresso machine be as noisy as it liked. But before I had a chance to foam the milk, the doorbell rang. I felt annoyed; it was my birthday, and no one was letting me ease myself into the day in peace. Yesterday's melancholy was still lying over my head like a dark cloud. It rang again, this time for longer. There was no post on Sundays, so it couldn't be that.

Charlotte was roused with a start. *Richard? Because of your birthday?*

I quickly pulled my bathrobe on, tried to smooth my hair down, tore open the front door, and pressed the buzzer. My heart had jumped into my mouth.

"It's your birthday!"

Dorothea, laden down with bags and flowers, was climbing up the stairs, beaming. Ines followed right behind her. "Good morning, sis, happy birthday!"

I looked back at them, trying to look excited and to keep Edith's mouth shut in my thoughts.

"Ines, Dorothea, it's not even nine a.m. yet."

Dorothea was the first to reach me, putting her bags down and hugging me.

"Happy birthday! You've achieved so much, and here's to it carrying on that way."

She kissed me on the mouth, then held me at arm's length, looked me up and down, and started to laugh.

"It's a good thing we're here early. Your hair is in a right state. And this bathrobe…"

Ines pushed us aside so she could close the apartment door. She shoved me right in front of the mirror and made me look. My hair was standing up in all directions and all fuzzy, and my red-checkered bathrobe was threadbare and longer in the front than the back.

I looked at Ines, shrugged my shoulders, and said, "Well, I'm forty now after all."

She laughed and gave me a big hug.

"Many happy returns, big sis. But you seem a little out of sorts—is the hour too early or your age too high?"

I answered as I followed Dorothea into the kitchen. "Both, and I haven't even had my first coffee yet."

For the next half hour I sat at the kitchen table, drank the coffee that Dorothea made for me, and watched in amazement as they took control of both my apartment and me. While Ines unpacked food and champagne bottles and tidied it all away into the fridge, Dorothea pulled her bags into the lounge while cheerfully humming "Happy Birthday." I could hear her rustling paper, moving the table, and clattering things about.

I lit up a cigarette and drank my coffee. They would tell me if they needed my help. By now, Ines had packed everything away and sat down next to me with fresh coffee. She smiled.

"Forty."

I smiled back. "When Mom was this old, I'd already finished my studies. That's the only strange thing."

Before we could get sentimental, Dorothea appeared in the kitchen doorway with her hands stretched out to the ceiling. "For she's a jolly good fellow, for she's a jolly…"

Ines interrupted her dodgy singing. "Are you done?"

Dorothea gave first her, then me, a sparkling smile.

"With the song, no not really, but if we don't have time then fine. Christine, you can look now."

My living room looked like the kind of birthday party any child would dream of. There were flowers and lit tea lights everywhere, the table was full of wrapped presents with Smarties sprinkled abundantly around them, and in the middle was a small cake, its candles burning brightly.

I was so moved that my eyes welled up and my throat felt itchy. Ines poked me.

"What's up? Do you want to cry or unwrap?"

It took almost half an hour to unwrap everything. Along with the gifts of hand cream for aging spots, shampoo for thinning hair, and eye cream, the kind I'd been using for ages without any visible success, I got a sinfully expensive handbag from Dorothea, a pair of earrings from Ines, a voucher for the beach sauna from my parents, and a ticket to the Hagenbeck Zoo from my brother. On the envelope Georg had written, "Just think, our last visit to the zoo together was thirty years ago."

I looked at Ines and Dorothea.

"It must be twenty years since anyone did all this for me on my birthday."

Ines shook her head gently.

"I was talking to Dorothea in the car already about what your birthdays were like in recent years. Do you remember? Bernd always had to work, his family arrived at eleven a.m. and stayed until ten p.m., and you just stood in the kitchen making food the whole time."

I could remember them clearly.

"I hated it. I was stocking up the food for a whole week beforehand and cleaning for three days before and three days after. I was always just happy when it was over."

Dorothea looked at me questioningly. "So why did you do it every year?"

I thought for a moment. "I never had the courage to do anything different. That was just how it was. For Bernd's birthday it was exactly the same thing all over again."

Dorothea waved the thought away. "Sweetheart, that's all in the past. Today you'll see what birthday parties are really about."

She looked at the clock. Ines followed her gaze.

"It's half past ten already. Christine, just concentrate on getting out of that bathrobe. Your guests will be arriving in an hour."

I'd completely forgotten about all the food and champagne.

"Who have you invited?"

Dorothea looked at me earnestly. "Bernd's whole family of course."

I looked back, stunned. But then she laughed. "That was just a bad joke, no, only nice people. Go and shower, and we'll get the table ready."

Two hours later my apartment had a real birthday atmosphere, full of the sound of voices and laughter. Ines and Dorothea had pulled the tables together and decorated them with flowers and candles, and in the kitchen there was an impressive buffet. Ines opened one bottle of champagne after the other.

I sat at the head of the table, feeling very special. To my right sat Georg, next to him Franziska, then Luise, then Marleen, who had phoned to wish me a happy birthday on her way to Hamburg, saying that she couldn't make it. Half an hour later she rang the bell.

Nina sat opposite, next to Maren and Rüdiger, then Leonie and Michael.

Dorothea and Ines were taking charge of serving the food as if they were professional waitresses. I sat at the head of the table, feeling guiltily like a diva. My offer of fetching drinks was turned down with the retort, "Sit down! You're forty and it's your birthday!"

The conversation was loud and lively, and everyone was talking to everyone. Marleen and Luise were meeting for the first time, but they had heard a lot about each other through me and immediately got onto the topic of real estate agents with little pink jackets. Leonie and Ines were reminiscing about the weirdest of the apartments they had checked out for me, Franziska and Nina were talking about a concert that one of them had been to and the other one wanted to see, Dorothea was talking at the top of her voice with Maren in the kitchen about men and women and in particular about my pending divorce. I joined in a little bit with everyone. When I realized that Rüdiger, Michael, and Georg were discussing TV rights, I felt a pang and thought of Richard.

Just at that moment, Franziska glanced over at me. She raised her eyebrows questioningly, and I smiled at her and stood up. Walking by, I laid my hand on her shoulder and whispered, "It's just my weak bladder."

She smiled and I went to the bathroom. Fetching my mobile from the chest of drawers in the hallway, I closed the door and sat down on the edge of the bathtub. No new messages. I looked back at the last text message.

"Birthday kiss. See you soon. Richard."

I brushed my thumb softly over the words.

"See you soon."

I missed him. I so wished that he could sit with us at the table, and I would have loved to introduce him to everyone.

I longed for his physical presence, for his stories, for the way he looked at me. In the next room sat the people who had helped me the most in these last months, and the person who was closest to my heart was missing. I'd told Richard everything about my friends and family, but they still didn't know anything about him. At that moment I would have done anything to be able to kiss him. I wanted to share the day, the people, the conversations with him. But he was in Berlin. With Sabine.

I felt a lump in my throat. Someone knocked on the door.

"Are you feeling ill? I have to go."

Marleen.

"Just a sec, I'm almost done."

I pushed my phone into my trouser pocket, pressed the flush lever, and washed my hands. When I came out, Marleen gave me a quick hug and looked at me questioningly.

"Is everything okay?"

My answer was rushed. "Of course, I'm just so touched that you're all here."

She stroked my cheek.

"Well, you've earned it. They're all great people."

I nodded proudly, waited as she shut the door behind her, and then went back to the others. As I sat back down in my chair, the conversation fell silent. Confused, I looked around me.

"Is something wrong? Did I come back too soon?"

Ten faces smiled at me.

Michael raised his glass. "Don't look so startled; I'm not going to make a speech. We were just talking about you, but only good things. You've been so amazing in the way you've stayed so composed through everything and…"

Leonie laid her hand on his arm and interrupted him.

"He says he's not making a speech, but it sounds like one. Many happy returns, Christine. Here's to your birthday, your new life, and…your composure."

Everyone raised their glasses, and Rüdiger cleared his throat. "On the topic of composure, as your lawyer you know I still think you're being far too nice when it comes to your soon-to-be ex-husband."

At that moment, Marleen came back to her seat and nodded in Rüdiger's direction.

"Oh yes, maybe she'll listen to you. I told her from the start that she's much too soft. Other women in Christine's position would have at least torched the house or terrorized Antje with venomous phone calls. But Christine just takes a few things and goes. No stress whatsoever."

Ines and I answered in unison. "Marleen."

We looked at each other. I carried on.

"It wouldn't have changed anything. As my grandmother always used to say, 'Behave in such a way that you can still talk about everything two years later without having to change the story.'"

Ines nodded. "The saying that came to my mind is 'You have to, and you can.'"

Maren groaned loudly. "The holier-than-thou family. Christine, my old man can really get some big bucks out of this for you if you want him to, and shoot dear old Bernd down while he's at it."

I shook my head. "People, please! I don't want to talk about this. It's fine as it is. I'm doing great, everything is much better than it was, and I have neither the time nor the inclination to prolong my old life. I want that chapter closed. Period. Now, can we change the subject please?"

Nina took up the suggestion. "Let's do that. Rüdiger's only making digs because your divorce won't just be quick, but also cheap."

She raised her glass at Rüdiger. He wagged his finger at her and made a play of looking distraught.

"It was just my opinion as a friend, nothing to do with work."

Nina ignored him. "So, new subject. Christine, you're almost done with all the stress now, so maybe it's time you started to focus on your love life again."

Charlotte whispered, *Richard.*

Edith answered, *Hold your tongue.*

Maren answered for me. "You'll have to leave that one to Christine, Nina. When it's meant to happen, it will happen."

Nina wouldn't let it go. "But you've been alone for eight months now. That must be horrible."

Dorothea started to laugh loudly. "My dear, I've been living alone for three years, and I still find it wonderful."

Ines stood up and collected the full ashtrays. "Now, let's change the subject, and by the way, it looks like we've emptied another bottle already."

Leonie tried to steer the conversation in another direction.

"Just don't settle down again too soon. Find a lover first, no strings, just for the transition period."

Seeing the uncomfortable expressions on Michael, Rüdiger, and Georg's faces, I stood up and followed

Ines into the kitchen. In passing, I said, "I'll think about it. By the way, there's still loads to eat. I'll fetch fresh plates."

In the kitchen Ines and Marleen were stacking the dishwasher. I started to wash the glasses by hand since they wouldn't fit in the machine. As Ines was about to protest, I interrupted her. "I have to do something; my bottom hurts from too much sitting down."

Franziska appeared next to me and grabbed a tea towel.

"Great idea. I'll take over kitchen duty with the birthday girl, and we'll be back before you know it."

Marleen looked at me questioningly. I nodded. "Let me hang out here for a moment. Why don't you open another bottle of champagne, and I'll bring it across. Besides, Ines has barely eaten anything while she's been serving everybody."

Ines looked at Marleen, then reached for a plate and helped herself to the buffet.

"Marleen, do you want some too?"

She did, so the two of them went back to the others with their plates piled high. Franziska silently polished the glasses that I put down for her. She glanced at me twice, and I had the feeling she wanted to ask me something. After the third glass, she did.

"Was Leonie serious about you finding a lover?"

"I think so. She already suggested it once when we were at the sauna."

Franziska energetically rubbed at the already dry glass. "That's unbelievable."

Astonished, I paused. I'd never seen Franziska as small-minded or excessively moral.

I tried to appease her. "Leonie doesn't want a lover for herself; she was just suggesting I should. I'm sure she didn't mean it that seriously."

Franziska took the next glass. "It's nothing against Leonie, I just think a suggestion like that is completely nuts."

I needed to summon all of my energy not to let Charlotte into my mind.

"Oh Franziska, come on, it's not like the streets of Hamburg are paved with lovers."

She looked at me earnestly. "Christine, I think it's great how you've coped these last months, and I'm really fond of you. You're perfectly entitled to tell me it's none of my business, but I was watching you earlier at the table and you looked sad a few times. And I saw you keep checking your cell phone. I'm sure you weren't waiting for a call from your ex, and when Leonie said that just now, alarm bells went off."

I put the glass down and looked at her. "What do you mean?"

She sat down at the kitchen table and thought for a moment before she answered.

"I could be wrong, perhaps it's just bringing back memories of my own experience, but don't start an affair with someone in your situation, especially not someone who's tied down."

I dried my hands and sat opposite her. "Is that what happened to you?"

Franziska looked at me. "Yes, and I'll never do it again. Back then I thought I could handle it, and that all the stuff about what lovers have to go through was just a cliché. You know, birthdays, weekends, Christmas—there are enough novels and films about it all. But unfortunately, every one of the clichés is true."

She paused and twisted her wedding ring. She saw my gaze fall on it. She looked up, smiled, and carried on.

"Eight years ago I was left just as despicably as you were. We weren't married and had only been living together for three years, but it was a shock to me nonetheless. Afterwards I moved from Münster to Hamburg. I wanted to get away and make a new start, and above all, never to fall in love again. I was here alone for a year, knew a few colleagues, some women from exercise classes and so on. Everything was peaceful and manageable. I often felt lonely, but I didn't mind.

"Over New Year I went on a skiing trip with my sister, and I met a man in the hotel there. His name was Hannes. He was a computer programmer and came from Hamburg. I thought he was amazing, and the feeling was mutual. He told me right away that he was married. His wife hated skiing, so he was there with a friend. Somehow, I was caught up in the moment back then and I didn't care. To cut to the chase, we got involved with each other. It was great, it was unbelievably easy, and we were enamored with one another.

"Three weeks after the trip, he turned up on my doorstep. His marriage was rather strange. His wife lived with the children in Munich, and he had been the manager of the Hamburg branch of a Munich software company for the last year. During the week he lived in Eppendorf, and on Fridays he flew to Munich. To start with I thought our situation was ideal. I didn't want a serious relationship, especially after the last debacle. We saw each other regularly and got along brilliantly. We hardly ever went away together in case we ran into people we knew. We kept things private, and that was enough for me. He was good for me."

I listened to her in fascination. Richard.

Franziska's eyes were sad.

"After a year it got more and more difficult. He had me, exclusively. There was nothing about me that he didn't know—job, friends, fears, family, emotions, even contracts and insurance policies. I only knew the Hamburg part of him. I had no idea what he was like in Munich with his family. You know, I always had to stay on my guard to make sure I didn't fall for him completely. Friday to Monday he was away, and I couldn't reach him; he left me there. Sometimes there would be a stolen phone call here and there, when he went shopping. I waited, for him to contact me, for him to come back to me from Munich on the spur of the moment; I was always waiting for something. I never let my cell phone out of my sight. I missed him so much, and it became more and more of a torment."

I was almost scared to ask. "Did you think he would leave her for you?"

Franziska thought about it. "Not for me, but perhaps with my help. He wasn't happy in his old life; we often spoke about that. After the first year he said to me that he wanted to get a divorce, that he felt so at ease with me and wanted to have that forever. In total, he said that five times, but it never happened. All I could do was wait. At some point I had the feeling that he only needed me to be able to endure his muddled life. I was making the very thing bearable that broke my heart every weekend. Plaster for the soul."

I saw Edith's triumphant smile. *Now, listen closely please. This is what happens.*

Charlotte seemed worried.

Franziska stood up and reached for the towel again. "It lasted two years; then he wanted to take a break, allegedly because I was finding the whole thing harder and harder to cope with. I had no more energy to fight him, so that's how it ended."

I stood beside her and washed the last two glasses. "What does Hannes do now?"

Franziska smiled bitterly. "He's working back in the Munich head office again. And is presumably a husband and father with a clear conscience."

My gaze fell on her wedding ring again. "So when did you meet Stefan?"

"I already knew him from before. He was one of my brother's colleagues. We were all celebrating New Year's together, and at midnight I had a crying fit about Hannes. Stefan came to my rescue. He was so caring, and that's how it happened. He's so different from Hannes, but he was there for me. It sounds silly, but you can't imagine how much I enjoyed just going to the supermarket with him. Everything was suddenly allowed—and simple."

I found her story unbearably sad. "How long ago was this?"

Her answer came quickly. "Five years. Shortly after that things with Stefan started, and we got married three years ago."

"Do you still think about Hannes?"

Franziska thought for a while. "Sometimes, when I hear certain songs and other memories come up. But it's always a sad feeling. Then I look at Stefan and feel that everything is safe and right. That calms me."

I felt a longing grow within me. And I felt Charlotte's fears at the same time. Before either of us could say anything, Dorothea ripped the door open.

"Are you guys laying contact paper in all the drawers or what? What's taking you so long?"

Franziska laughed. "That's an idea. Contact paper. Does that even still exist? We're done now."

She pushed me out of the kitchen and whispered, "I hope you didn't take that the wrong way. It's just that it was very hard for me at times, and I would prefer to spare you from feeling the same thing. But if you're not sure, then don't pay too much attention to the bitter ramblings of a middle-aged woman."

I let her go ahead of me, watching her walk away. At that moment my cell rang. My heart pounded when I saw the name on the display. Richard. I answered the call and went back into the kitchen.

"Christine, I at least wanted to congratulate you myself. Many happy returns on your birthday. I'm kissing and hugging you."

I could hear strange noises in the background.

"Thank you. I'm kissing you too. Where are you?"

There was so much clattering and rattling that I could hardly hear him.

"I'm just bringing the bottles to the recycling. They're making such a racket."

Edith whispered, *Stolen conversations.*

I swallowed. Then I heard his voice again, and it went straight to my heart.

"Have you had a nice day?"

"Ines and Dorothea invited lots of guests over. It's lovely, but you're not here."

Richard's voice was hesitant. "Yes, I know, but it wouldn't be possible. I have to go now. Will it wait until Wednesday?"

I answered quickly. "Of course, seven p.m. at your place. I'm looking forward to it a lot."

Richard's voice was tender now. "Me too. And we'll celebrate your birthday in style. See you soon. Enjoy the rest of your day."

We hung up.

I took a deep breath and went back to my birthday guests.

We sat together for another few hours, ate a lot, drank a lot, and talked without stopping. I couldn't remember the last time I'd had so much fun with this many guests. Richard's call had set my heart at ease, and the people here, my mind.

As the evening approached, the party began to draw to a close. Marleen had taken the next day off and was staying at my place for the night, so I said sentimental goodbyes to the others. Ines and Dorothea offered their help cleaning up, which Marleen and I refused.

"We'll manage. I've hardly spoken with Christine yet, and you get to see her in Hamburg all the time. Leave us alone this once."

I hugged Dorothea and Ines. "Thank you, both of you, that was the most wonderful birthday I've had in years."

They were the last guests to leave. As the door closed behind them, Marleen and I were left alone. We looked around us in the apartment and took a deep breath at the sight of the chaos. Marleen pulled her sleeves up and looked at me.

"Come on, let's make a start. We'll get things shipshape now, and then we can open up the champagne I brought."

An hour later we were sitting in the tidied and cleaned kitchen with a cooler holding an open bottle of champagne between us. We had lit candles, and there were vases full of flowers everywhere. I felt good, the day had been great, my apartment was beautiful, I had only had people around me whom I liked, and they had all liked each other too. It was easy and undemanding in a way that I hadn't experienced for ages.

Marleen stretched out her legs, reached for my cigarettes, and lit one up.

"I only ever smoke when I'm drinking with you. I really should bring you a box sometime."

I pushed an ashtray towards her. "Don't you dare!"

Marleen smiled and looked at me. "Are you proud?"

I thought about the question. "Of myself? I don't know. I'm proud of all the people who were here, I know that. It's good for me, this new life of mine."

Marleen poured champagne. "I told you, didn't I? That we'd be laughing about it on your birthday. And I'm certainly proud of you." She raised her glass at me.

We both drank and fell into a peaceful silence. Images flew through my head: Marleen and I in her house on the day when she told me everything, Bernd and I on her terrace, the bottle bank, the mailbox application, Luise and Stilwerk, and then suddenly, Richard.

I felt Marleen watching me. When I looked up, she asked me.

"Now, tell me what's going on. Something's up with you. I wanted to ask you weeks ago on the phone, but you always dodge the question. Where are you on Wednesdays, for example? I can never get hold of you then. I realized that last month."

I looked at her, heard Franziska's voice in my mind, took a deep breath, and started. "Six years ago I met one of Bernd's colleagues in Berlin. His name is Richard."

I told her the whole story, making an effort to keep everything in the right chronological order and to relay it in a factual voice. I only hinted at my feelings, but I did describe him, recount some of the many funny things he'd said, and talked about his job, his apartment, his life.

It did me good to talk about him.

When I finished, Marleen took another cigarette. I couldn't read her facial expression. I tried to preempt a possible judgment.

"Marleen, I know what you're going to say. I'm getting involved in someone else's marriage, I'm no better than Antje, it will all end in tears, after all my experiences I shouldn't be someone's lover, I…"

Looking amazed, she interrupted me. "You have no idea what I'm going to say. Perhaps you could let me speak for myself?"

"Sorry, I take it back."

Marleen smiled and thought for a moment. "I saw your face when you were talking about him. And I read between the lines a little. The rest doesn't really matter to me. If it's doing you good, if he makes your heart race and you feel alive again, then let it be. It's right for now."

I thought about Franziska's story and her warning. "When I was in the kitchen with Franziska before, she told me her story to scare me off. Before she met her husband she was having an affair with a married man for three years. She suffered a lot, and I found the story quite depressing."

Marleen waved that aside. "That was her story, not yours. It's nonsense too. What do you want to make plans for at this stage? You're in love, Richard seems to be too, and so what? As long as you're okay, it's the best thing that could happen to you right now. You can build up your new life here in peace, but have something for your heart and your desires too. So just wait and see."

Edith butted in. *You can't plan anything. You have to share him. You're the other woman.*

As if Marleen had heard Edith, she answered. "You're coming out of a supposedly dependable, planned relationship. When was the last time someone made your heart pound? Five years ago? Ten? That's a real shame. What you have, right now, doesn't come along very often."

Charlotte thanked her quietly.

I wasn't so sure. "I don't know. My heart says yes, but my head says no."

Marleen shared out the rest of the champagne between our glasses. She looked me straight in the eyes. "Christine, then listen to your heart and let yourself go. You can rely on your head; after all, you've achieved enough. But you haven't *lived* enough in the last few years, that's my opinion. You're forty, you're independent, you've set up a wonderful life for yourself, and Richard is just the icing on the cake.

And even if it goes wrong, you can laugh about this in half a year's time as well. So, I'm happy for you. Just let it be."

I drank down the rest of the champagne.

Edith retreated. Charlotte smiled.

I caught Marleen's eye. "I thought my life would be more peaceful and well-ordered now."

She looked at me, pretending to be horror-struck. "Heaven forbid. That would be awful."

As I lay in bed later, my thoughts turned to Richard. So, I thought, we'll just let it happen.

Moments later, I fell fast asleep.

Couples

I t was December 23, and I was in a good mood. At least, that was my intention.

The car radio was playing the eternally popular Christmas hits, and the Christmas lights on the houses and streets put to rest any dark thoughts. I had an amazingly tender night behind me and days of festivities in Sylt in front of me. I turned the volume up as Chris Rea sang "Driving Home for Christmas" and drove along the highway towards Hamburg.

Richard and I had had our Christmas meal the night before. He was now on his way to Berlin, and I was driving to my parents'. The two highways separated in Hamburg. I joined the long line of cars driving northwards.

The radio presenter was talking in her professionally jolly voice about some jolly event at a Christmas market in Harz organized by Radio NDR, and she said that—as a result—the traffic jam near the Walsroder triangle was now backed up to twenty-one kilometers. Reassured, I turned the volume down—it wasn't on my route—and then I turned it right back up again as Dido sang "White Flag," from the album we'd listened to for half the night.

I saw Richard's face in front of me. He had such a particular way of looking at me when I was getting undressed. Tender, full of desire, and a little lustful. I loved that look. I also loved what came after it.

The brake lights on the Opel Zafira in front of me suddenly lit up. I braked too, went to fifty, then thirty, and then came to a standstill.

Dido was blended out by the jolly NDR voice that cheerfully announced that there was now very slow-moving traffic for twenty-five kilometers on the A1 between the Bremen crossing and Stuckenborstel.

Great, I thought. But I still had time. And I was in a good mood.

The driver of the Opel laid his hand on his passenger's neck. He said something to her, and she looked at him and laughed. Then she stroked his cheek and bent over and kissed him.

I cleared my throat and lit up a cigarette.

My separation was now ten months ago, and there was no doubt that my life had changed for the better since then. I felt at home in Hamburg, I liked my circle of girlfriends, I had more money, more freedom, more self-confidence, and I was in love again. But despite that there were still moments when I felt alone.

Last weekend Leonie and Michael had asked me over for a pre-Christmas coffee. I really liked the way they were in each other's company. They never walked past each other without a brief touch or caress. After fifteen years they still looked at each other proudly and winked at one another.

The traffic was beginning to move, slowly.

My thoughts wandered back to Richard. When he stood up from the table we had been sitting at for hours, talking about the world, he went around the back of my chair and kissed me on the neck. I felt a small shiver.

I turned my concentration back to the highway. I drove slowly along the route on autopilot. For the last three months I'd been visiting Richard regularly, first in the hotel, then at his apartment, first just on Wednesdays, and now as often as we could. The small apartment in Bremen had become an important part of my new life, and I was happy each time I went.

Edith tried to push Richard's face from my mind. *And every weekend you're sad because your wonderful guy is with his wife in Berlin. You guys aren't Leonie and Michael, remember; you're having an affair.*

Charlotte answered. *So what? As long as you feel good with him, it's all fine. On weekends you have time for your girlfriends, for single life in the big city, for you. Not many people can have both; that's a good thing.*

Edith disagreed. *You have no choice in the matter; it's not your decision. And to top it off, if you'd driven to Sylt from Hamburg as you'd planned, you wouldn't be sitting in this damn traffic jam now.*

I felt a headache coming on and reminded myself it was the holidays.

Richard and I had eaten in an enchanting restaurant, walking back through the clear, starry, and cold night to his apartment afterwards, and then we drank another bottle of champagne at his place while undressing each other. Slowly and with endless pleasure.

Charlotte had a smile in her voice. *And this morning you woke up to his caresses. He was right there beside you, and he didn't want to let you leave.*

Edith wouldn't give up. *But he did, because he had to go as well. And now you're driving to Sylt alone.*

By now I had a full-on headache and was starting to need the bathroom. After a short while I saw the sign: "Ostetal, 1000 meters."

I put my turn signal on and drove into the parking lot. There was a bustling holiday atmosphere, something I really liked about service stations. Families with their cars packed with suitcases and Christmas presents, young people, who despite now having their own lives still went home for the holidays and were beaming with a little excited anticipation, mothers who shouted loudly that Kevin and Anastasia had to go to the bathroom now.

Washing my hands in the restroom between all the Kevins and Anastasias, I looked at myself in the big mirror.

Not bad at all, I thought. Relaxed posture, good clothes, good mood. That's what you must look like when you've had sex three hours ago. This man was doing me good. And he made me beautiful. Charlotte smiled, and Edith stayed silent.

Before long I was heading for a free table in the cafeteria with coffee, rolls, and water for my headache pills.

You're the only one who's sitting here alone. Everyone else is with their loved ones.

I swallowed Edith's accusatory voice down with the tablet.

At the next table someone was sitting with their loved one. Both were in their mid forties, and they sat opposite one another, sharing breakfast from a tray between them. Judging by their faces, they were sharing for financial rather than romantic reasons. She looked at him through narrow eyes...but he didn't bother to look at her at all. They weren't talking. They had probably been married for twenty years and were so saturated with the mundane nature of daily life and had so few real conversations that they no longer had any idea whether they even liked each other. Togetherness at any price.

It made me think of Nina.

We hadn't seen much of each other in recent weeks; the sports center that we played squash in had been closed for the last month for renovations. Last Friday Nina had phoned me. She suggested that we meet up at the Christmas market in the town hall square for some mulled wine; otherwise, we wouldn't see each other until the New Year.

As I walked up to where we were meeting, she was already waiting for me. She was in high spirits, her eyes sparkling, and after a short hello her news came rushing out.

"Christine, I've met someone. His name is Thomas, and it's so wonderful."

I was surprised, but happy for her. "Where did you meet, and when?"

She seemed elated. "I put an ad in the *Scene*, you know, the local magazine. Just imagine, I got forty-two responses; of course lots of them were useless, too young, too old, married, I'm sure you get the picture. But Thomas was one of them. Right age, no baggage, taller than me. We had a coffee date in Blankenese by the river, very romantic, and since then it's all been great."

That's quick, I thought and asked, "Okay, so what's he like? What does he do?"

Fidgeting, Nina pushed her hair back under her hat. "Well, he's a civil servant, something in the transport office. He sails, he loves Formula One, and has lots of hobbies. The most important thing is that he's had enough of single life and wants a serious relationship."

I was baffled. Nina got seasick and hated Michael Schumacher. I tried to look enthusiastic. "That's great. So when do I get to meet this Prince Charming?"

Nina looked a little strained. "Oh, let's do that in the New Year. But Christine, just so you don't get the wrong idea, he's not the most good-looking of men, and you probably shouldn't talk about books with him—he's not really interested in that kind of thing."

Now I was amazed. "But Nina, books are your job, so he should at least show an interest. How he looks doesn't really matter."

She laughed, a little falsely. "Oh, I'll get him onto reading at some point; I'm sure he can manage a little of it. But apart from that it's really great. Over New Year we're going to the East Frisian Islands together."

Togetherness at any price.

I was just as depressed by Nina's obsessive goal to end her single life as I was by the silent couple next to me. They weren't thinking about their feelings; perhaps they didn't even have any for one another anymore. They got their satisfaction elsewhere—new furniture, a new car, two weeks in Mallorca. Vacationing together was agony, and out of the stifling boredom and frustrated arguments would come the inevitable postcard summary: "Great weather, great food. Best wishes."

What Richard and I had was so much better after all. We saw each other because we wanted to, our conversations lasted hours, we listened to one another, held one another, desired each other's body and soul. Not a single minute was wasted.

Edith had to have her say. *You don't see each other when you want to, you see each other when it suits him. This isn't just about feelings.*

Charlotte replied, *But there are a lot of feelings here. He's the best thing that's ever happened to you; he does you good. Look at the couple next to you. Do you want that instead?*

I stood up and took my tray back. On the way to my car I found myself thinking about Anke and Werner. They had been married for twenty years, fourteen of which Anke had had younger lovers for. Whenever they make her feel too old, she just goes back to Werner, feels younger again because of their twenty-year age gap, and then the whole game starts all over again.

Werner suffers but doesn't dwell on it, buys one house after the other, increases his wealth for all to see, and that's how he gets his legitimacy. His fear of a new life was clearly bigger than his suffering in his current one. I shook these miserable stories from my mind, turned the key in the ignition, and rejoined the highway.

Richard's face pushed its way back into my thoughts.

We always slept entwined in one another, my back against his stomach, his hand on my breast. I could still feel the warmth of his skin, his steady breathing on the back of my neck. As soon as I drove away from him, I missed him.

The feeling of longing overcame me, followed by a wave of sadness. I turned the volume on the car radio back up and tried to capture some childlike anticipation for the family festivities to come with the help of the cheerful Christmas songs. I almost managed it.

But Edith stepped in. *You're not a child anymore, and you're missing Richard already. You're not going to see him again for three whole weeks.*

The wave of sadness grew.

My cell phone saved me from my crumbling attempt to control my thoughts. I pressed the green button, and Dorothea's voice came through the hands-free speaker.

"It's me. Where are you?"

"I'm almost exactly halfway between Bremen and Hamburg on my way to Sylt."

"Oh yes, you're going today. Why Bremen? Oh, were you with Richard?"

I had told Dorothea about him four weeks ago. Dorothea loved hearing about people's love lives, and she was excited for me. She reacted similarly to Marleen and brushed away any misgivings. "Life is too short to be unhappy in love. Just enjoy it."

"Yes, I was at Richard's. It was the last time I'll see him for the next three weeks."

The longing mounted again.

Dorothea laughed. "Oh, come on, you'll hardly have time to miss him. Once you get back from Sylt there'll be Luise's 'Between the Years' party, then it'll be New Year's Eve, then we have to get through all the vouchers for saunas, makeovers, and cinema that I get from my mother each year for Christmas. Believe me, there'll be so much to do that you wouldn't have time to go to Bremen anyway."

I took a deep breath.

Before I could say a word, Dorothea carried on. "It'll be lovely. I'm off work until the tenth of January too, and we've hardly seen each other recently. You're always with Richard. Just kidding! Anyway, he'll be missing you too; you're not the only one. And that's the good thing about it, looking forward to seeing each other, no moaning or squabbling, no mundane daily life, just champagne, sex, and butterflies in your stomach."

Dorothea's confidence filled the whole car.

My voice became more lighthearted. "Was Nils with you?"

Dorothea sighed contentedly before she said, "Yes, for five days. It was divine, but to be honest I'm happy that he's gone now too. His things were everywhere in my apartment; I'm not used to such close proximity."

Dorothea had a three-bedroom apartment. I started to laugh.

"You poor thing. Well, now you've got free reign for your quirks. I hope you have a wonderful Christmas, and give your family my love."

"Sweetheart, the same back at you. Drive safely, kiss all the Santa Clauses you can, and I'll look forward to seeing you next week. Until then, bye!"

I pressed the button on the hands-free and the radio kicked back in.

"Last Christmas." I must have heard this song playing on the way to Sylt every year for the last twenty years.

Over the next hour I gave in to my thoughts. About Richard, about couples, about love, about Christmas. I'd just gone through the Elbe Tunnel when Luise phoned.

"Hello, Christine. Are you already on the island?"

"Luise! No, I'm still en route. And you?"

"I'm at home. I've just got back from shopping, and for the first time in my life I just bought a Christmas tree and dragged it here all by myself. I'm really proud."

Picturing her slim figure, I was suspicious about the size of the tree.

"I thought you were going to your father's place in Berlin? Are you at home by yourself?"

I heard a smile in her voice. "Actually, that's what I was calling to tell you about. No, I cancelled going to Berlin. I met up with Alex two weeks ago. It was really amazing, and he's coming this evening and staying until New Year. So you'll get to meet him next week."

"Luise, that's great! Are you happy?"

"More than I have been in years. I'll tell you the rest next week. I have to start cooking now. We'll see each other on Friday at my place. I'm looking forward to it. Oh yes, and merry Christmas!"

"The same to you, have a wonderful few days. See you next week."

As I hung up I felt happy for Luise, and the longing for Richard came back.

My gaze fell on the fuel gauge. I would have to make another stop at the next rest station. By now I was already past Schleswig. When I saw the sign for the Hüttener Berge rest stop, I put the turn signal on and joined the right lane.

There was a line in front of the gas pumps. It was the last gas station before the Danish border, so I joined the line, a little irritated, but there was nothing else I could do. Three cars were in front of me, so I turned the engine off and rolled the window down. Suddenly I heard the squeal of brakes and saw a Mercedes, driven by a woman who had just cut in front of a minibus.

There was no crash, but despite that a hefty argument kicked off between the woman and her passenger. He was gesticulating wildly at her with an enraged expression. Her answer was just as forceful; she got out, went around the car, and ripped the passenger door open. He jumped out, pushed her brusquely aside, and then she got back in, and I could still hear her loud and angry voice.

"I've had enough! I've had it up to here with you!"

The man sat behind the steering wheel, turned the engine back on, and drove off aggressively.

I watched them go and wondered where their anger was coming from. How could an incident like that, where nothing had really happened, provoke so much rage and contempt?

I had bypassed the stage in my marriage when love turns first to indifference and then to contempt. Perhaps the only reason things with Richard were so good was because it wasn't real life. Perhaps I was doing everything wrong all over again.

Charlotte shook her head. *You two talk about everything. You're honest with one another. You help each other. You have a strong erotic connection and an open spiritual connection. That's happiness. Sometimes it can work.*

It was my turn, so I got out and filled the car with gas.

Edith wasn't convinced. *So why are you standing here alone? Where's the happiness in that?*

Charlotte held her ground. *Better to be happy sometimes than constantly in danger of being looked at with such rage and contempt.*

I was still mumbling this sentence to myself as I went up to pay. The man at the counter looked at me, surprised. "Sorry?"

"Oh, I mean, merry Christmas."

He nodded at me blankly. "Yes, same to you."

It was starting to snow as I left the highway. The last four kilometers to Niebüll were on country roads. The radio was playing "White Christmas" now, as the snowfall got heavier and the road got slippery. I had to concentrate and had no time for thoughts or voices. Before long, I reached the car embarkation area and drove slowly onto the motorail. Once my car was parked and the engine off, I leaned back on the headrest, relieved. I hated driving on black ice.

The motorail slowly set off.

Edith was back in a flash. *If something had happened to you back there, you wouldn't even have been able to reach Richard.*

Charlotte answered. *But before you left, he said this morning in a very concerned and tender voice, "Look after yourself. I'm looking forward to the eighth of January." And he really meant it.*

Edith's voice was spiteful. *"Look after yourself." What else is he supposed to say? He hasn't even phoned to ask how the journey's going. Out of sight, out of mind. You have to look after yourself; otherwise, you're going to end up getting hurt in all this.*

Call me, Richard, I thought, with a fervor that surprised even me.

When I left that morning, he had stood in the doorway, naked and smiling at me. The memory of it made my knees feel weak.

It's love, said Charlotte.

It's already starting to hurt. Think about Franziska, said Edith.

I looked at the sea—cut in two by the Hindenburg Dam. Watching the water calmed me.

Perhaps they were all right. Edith in that the feelings between Richard and I wouldn't be enough to change the things that needed to be changed. Charlotte in that you're lucky to experience something like this and you need to approach it with patience and love. Franziska in that love without a future can be agony. Nina in that you can only conquer loneliness with a partner. Luise in that we deserve the best and shouldn't settle for any less. Dorothea in that we can only rely on ourselves. Marleen in that everything will happen as it's meant to.

We rolled onto the island, the windows steamed up with the cold.

I thought I'd come to understand life, but at that moment I had no idea what it was doing to me. Some things were good for me, but others caused me pain. I would find out with time.

My cell rang. The name I'd been waiting for was on the display.

I pressed the green button and heard the softness of his voice.

"Are you okay?"

Edith stayed silent, and Charlotte hummed Dido.

I had to think for a moment to find the right answer. "I think so, yes."

We spoke for a while. Once the conversation was over, I had his voice in my ears and the picture of his face in my mind. He was the best thing that could have happened to me. I felt alive with him. I reminded myself of what Marleen had said.

"When was the last time someone made your heart pound?"

It happened all the time now. And it was good.

"Enjoy what you have. And if it all goes wrong, you can laugh about it in half a year's time."

She was right. Everything would happen as it was meant to.

The train had come to a halt. So had my thoughts.

Letting Go

The church tower clock struck ten as I drove my car into the space in front of the district court. I was exactly one hour too early. I'd allowed myself to be driven mad by one of the sentences in the official summons letter.

"The personal attendance of the parties is compulsory."

It was terrifying, but then I had never had any intention of not being present. As I lay in bed the previous night, horror scenarios had run through my mind. Traffic hold-ups, flooded streets, closed roads, accidents, detours without rerouting signs. I wondered what the consequences would be if I couldn't be there in person.

Then I had put the light back on and set my alarm for an hour earlier.

It wasn't necessary; I fell asleep around four a.m. and woke up again just before six. Still in my bathrobe, I drank three cups of coffee. When I noticed my hands shaking, I made myself a pot of herbal tea. With my cup in my hand, I then stood in front of my closet for an hour, wondering what kind of clothes were appropriate for an appointment like this.

First, I went to shower, then drank more tea and smoked five cigarettes. Keeping an eye on the time all the while.

At around seven thirty I started to get worked up. I was freezing, wearing just my underwear as I searched for something to wear. I finally decided on a gray trouser suit, which I'd bought for the going away party of one of my work colleagues, together with a red blouse. Looking at my reflection in the mirror it occurred to me that red was an aggressive color. So I took the jacket back off, swapped it for a black roll-neck pullover, and put the jacket back on.

I felt content with what I saw in the mirror. I looked businesslike and grown-up, but on closer inspection I realized I'd forgotten to put my makeup on. Taking the jacket off yet again, I put some on with shaking hands. Hopefully it would only be noticeable close-up that my eyeliner was crooked; it would have to do.

At eight a.m. I was ready to go and set off in the car. The temperature was almost mild for the end of February, and the streets were clear. It was a dry day, and when I left the highway an hour later driving towards the North Sea, I noticed that the first crocuses were starting to appear in the gardens.

The worst part is over, I thought, not knowing whether I meant the winter or something else.

I turned my thoughts to the appointment I had in one of the bookstores at two this afternoon. I had told my other three clients that I would have to postpone due to a private appointment, which hadn't been a problem. But I would be able to make the two o'clock easily; the booksellers were nice, and it was on my way back. Then it would be the start of the weekend. I wondered what to do, maybe go to the cinema or out for a meal with Luise.

Edith took a deep breath, so I turned the radio up.

"Please, not now," I said, startled that I was speaking out loud yet again.

The journey had lasted about two hours, as always. As there were no floods or diversions, I now had an hour to kill. My stomach churned. I was unsure whether it was hunger or nerves, but either way it didn't feel good.

Opposite the court there was a bakery with a café. When Bernd and I used to go shopping together on the weekend, we would sometimes have coffee there. I locked my car, put my jacket over my arm, and went into the bakery. The woman at the counter was still the same. She smiled at me as I walked in.

"Hello, well, I haven't seen you in a long while. How are you? You must be sending your husband off to do the shopping, and quite right too. Cup of coffee?"

I smiled, strained, and swallowed down an honest answer. She probably didn't want to hear one anyway. "Yes please, a cup of coffee and a cheese roll."

Two more customers came in and put an end to any more chat.

I balanced my tray on the counter by the wall and stirred my coffee, keeping the district court in my sight. It was a beautiful building, and I'd never noticed it before, but then I hadn't had any reason to. Today I did.

Just looking at the slice of gherkin on the cheese roll made me feel ill. I pushed it aside and noticed that the cheese was lighter underneath. My stomach churned again, and it definitely wasn't from hunger.

The case about to be heard was a matter of family law. At least, that's what it said in the letter, which wasn't a normal letter, but a summons. I didn't feel like it was to do with me. Bernd and I were suddenly two opposing parties who had been summoned to a divorce proceeding.

We had fallen in love, moved in together, married, grown apart, hurt each other, and then finally separated. Bernd and I were involved in it all and had made all these decisions by ourselves. And yet suddenly it was a matter of law and we had to justify our decisions to strangers.

I felt nauseous and dizzy. I left my tray and fled from the bakery. The likelihood of my ever drinking coffee here again was very slim, and it didn't matter what the woman thought of me. Outside, I took a deep breath. The dizziness started to subside. I looked at the time. Ten twenty. Another forty minutes of being a wife.

A black BMW with Hamburg plates swung into the parking lot.

I felt relieved. Rüdiger. I already had my new life; this was all just a formality. It didn't matter.

When he got out and came towards me, it became more and more real. I'd never seen him in a suit, and he was carrying a black barrister's robe over his arm. He stretched his hand out to me. I shook it, feeling my legs shaking. He looked at me.

"Well, Christine, it's nearly all over."

I took a deep breath. "I had hoped I'd be feeling cooler about it."

He smiled and shook his head. "A divorce is a divorce. But if it makes you feel better, I've done much worse ones, you know. Yours is relatively simple. Is the opposing party already here?"

I flinched. "I haven't seen Bernd yet. Oh, Rüdiger, it all sounds so serious. I feel ill."

He grabbed my elbow and pulled me towards the entrance.

"It is serious, and that's a good thing. Come on, you've done so well so far; don't give in on me at the last hurdle."

At that moment we heard a car horn. Bernd's car drove in and pulled up next to Rüdiger's. The passenger door opened and Stefan, one of his sailing friends, got out. I was just wondering why he was here when it occurred to me that Stefan was a lawyer. Bernd's lawyer.

Rüdiger and I stayed put. I leaned towards him and said, "The opposing party." I thought it was silly, and I waited for someone to say, "That wasn't serious, just a joke."

Bernd smiled at me and seemed alarmingly familiar in this strange scene. Then it seemed to occur to him where he was. His facial expression became forcibly serious. Stefan looked embarrassed. Just a year ago we had been socializing together.

Rüdiger diffused the situation. With practiced professionalism, he gave Stefan his hand and introduced himself. He nodded briefly at Bernd, then looked at his watch and said, "Let's go in."

I walked up the stairs alongside Bernd. Apart from an awkward hello, we hadn't spoken to one another. We followed our lawyers. I observed myself, then Bernd. He looked just like he always did; he was wearing the blue shirt that I'd bought him for his last birthday. I wondered whether he even realized. The courtrooms were on the first floor. We stopped in front of courtroom twelve. Rüdiger fell in beside me, and Bernd went to stand alongside Stefan. There were about five meters between us. I forced myself not to look at Bernd, positioned myself with my back to him and looked at Rüdiger. I couldn't think of anything to say.

Rüdiger nodded to me. "It will all be quick. Don't worry, just leave it all to me." As he spoke, he pulled his robe on. I nodded to him thankfully. Then froze. The door was flung open and a young woman called our names out. Rüdiger went into the room first with me following. It looked like a proper courtroom, only smaller and shabbier. My lawyer sat on the right-hand side, pulling a chair alongside him for me. As I sat down, I felt myself shaking.

The four of us sat silently in this strange room for several minutes. It was unreal.

Then another door was opened up and the judge appeared. Rüdiger tapped my elbow, and we stood up briefly before sitting back down again. As the judge began to read out our names, talking about the facts of the case, the state of affairs and legal positions, alimony, the right to appeal, and family law licenses, my thoughts started to wander. I heard Rüdiger say something, looked at Bernd, then Stefan and the judge, but I was somewhere else entirely. Rüdiger nudged me throughout; I had to say yes twice. I did it without knowing why.

The judge read out his statement into a Dictaphone. After every paragraph he played the recording back in order to repeat his comments. The speed of the tape must have been set wrongly or was faulty because the voice sounded like it was on helium.

Suddenly I found the situation so absurd that I felt a fit of laughter swelling within me. Rüdiger noticed and touched me lightly. "Almost over," he murmured. I pulled myself together and noticed from the corner of my eye that Bernd was watching me. I didn't return his gaze. Then we had to stand up; I didn't know what to expect.

"The following verdict is now pronounced. In the name of the people..."

I struggled for air and only heard snippets of sentences. "...concluded in front of the registrar...the marriage of the parties is dissolved...the value of the proceedings..."

I was divorced in the name of the people. I looked at Rüdiger, then across at the other side. I didn't know what to think. It hadn't even lasted half an hour, as long as a short movie. The judge shook the lawyers' hands, nodded briefly to Bernd and me, and then left the room through one door while we went through another.

We stopped in the hallway, hesitating. Stefan was the first to speak. "Shall we go out for coffee perhaps?"

I stared at him. Surely that kind of thing only happened in the movies.

Rüdiger was quicker. "That would be nice, wouldn't it, Christine? Do you have time? Would you like to?"

I had no idea.

Bernd pulled his jacket on. "Yes, come on, I've got time for a quick coffee too."

Like a lemming, I followed Rüdiger. We walked two blocks to where there was a small bistro, one I had been to once with Marleen. After we'd got our drinks, Stefan and Rüdiger talked first about the judge, then about the court. Then Stefan looked at me.

"So how are you? Have you settled into Hamburg?"

My feeling of numbness was slowly subsiding. "Yes, I have. It's all worked out wonderfully."

Bernd looked at his watch and then at me. "Are you driving straight back?"

"I've got an appointment on my way back."

Rüdiger laughed. "Always so hard-working. You're not slacking off even today?"

I had no desire to explain how this had been hanging over me and that my appointment was the only way I could think of for getting some normality back in the day. So I just nodded.

Rüdiger looked for his briefcase. "I have to make a move now though. Marleen and I have been invited to a wedding, and I need to pop back to the office first."

Stefan waved him aside. "Put your money away, I'll get this."

We waited for the bill and then got up to leave. Rüdiger and I walked a few steps ahead. He leaned over to me. "Now it's behind you. Is it a good feeling?"

I tried to figure out how I felt. "I'm slowly starting to feel relieved, yes, really good, I think."

He winked at me. "You see. Now, I really have to make a move and see whether the couple at this evening's wedding make a better job of it! Come on, that was just a joke. You could even marry again right away if you want to; it's all legal now."

Stefan and Bernd were standing next to us. Rüdiger shook their hands, then got into his car and drove off. I said goodbye to Stefan, who was climbing into Bernd's car. Bernd seemed a little awkward.

"So, Christine, take care. Let's speak on the phone sometime."

He leaned forward clumsily and kissed the air next to my ear.

Unspeakable, I thought. And I felt a little sad.

I noticed that he was watching me as I walked over to my car. Sitting in my car and driving towards Hamburg, I waited for the waves of emotion to take hold. But nothing happened. The hearing just felt like it was some movie I had seen. The unreal feeling was still there. It had nothing to do with my real life; it had just been a formality. The hurt, the grieving, the fears, and new beginnings had all taken place a year ago. Away from the prying eyes of the "people" and the court. I felt light; I was happy to have finally drawn a line under it all.

An hour later I drove into the parking lot at the bookstore. I wasn't exactly on time; I'd underestimated the weekend traffic. As I walked into the shop, the otherwise lovely bookseller seemed annoyed.

"I cut my lunch break short especially for this meeting, and then you arrive half an hour late. That's so unlike you. I'm a little irritated, to be honest."

I apologized, unpacked my paperwork, sat down at the table, and smiled at her.

But she wasn't done. "And it's not just that—something went wrong with the last order. Mrs. Peterson wanted to discuss it with you, but she wasn't able to wait. That's not good either."

I wanted to stay polite, but the nerve-wracking demands of the day were slowly taking their toll. My voice remained calm.

"Mrs. Schmidt, I'm half an hour late. I am sorry, but I really couldn't make it any sooner."

"Then you shouldn't arrange your appointments so close to one another."

I still stayed calm. "There wasn't any other way around it today."

"Yes, yes, I know. I guess it was some big chain bookstore. You don't care about the small booksellers—it's fine to be late with them."

"It was a court case."

"What?"

"I had my divorce hearing at eleven a.m. In the name of the people. I've come directly from there."

Mrs. Schmidt started. She opened her mouth, shut it again, sat down slowly, put her hands to her cheeks, and looked at me guiltily.

I was almost sorry to have shocked her like this. Hurriedly, I said that it had just been a formality, the separation was a year ago, and I was doing fine. But she wanted to know more anyway. I answered in a friendly way, and it sounded like I was talking about one of the books I was presenting to her. "It was the banal story of two people who fit together for a while and then realized they'd made a mistake. And who then separated unspectacularly and without any major drama. The divorce was just like the marriage itself."

The appointment lasted two hours. By the end Mrs. Schmidt had calmed down and I was back in my normal life.

On my way back home I thought about the banal story. You really could describe it like that. We had made a mistake. It's just that we didn't notice for the first few years, as we still had shared goals back then that glossed over it. Bernd's studies, my job, our first vacation, our first purchases, the house. When all that was accomplished, all we had left was each other. And that hadn't been enough for either of us.

I thought about Richard. We weren't seeing each other as often anymore because of my work schedule and his appointments. But when we did see each other, it was amazing. I'd never had such intense evenings and nights with Bernd. There were however strict rules, which meant that he was only there for me during the week in Bremen and not contactable at other times.

Sometimes I found playing by these rules difficult, and sometimes the longing was stronger. When I was away from him I would think now and then of Franziska and feel alone, but then Charlotte would remind me of my boring and conversation-less marriage.

"What you have with Richard is still miles better, even if you don't have it that often. And in any case, the rest of your life is just as great."

Usually, I would then give Luise or Dorothea a call.

I drove past a highway sign: "Hamburg, 49 km." I was divorced and lived in Hamburg. That sounded good. I was surprised at how lighthearted I felt. The divorce really hadn't unleashed any great emotions. I dialed Luise's number. After four rings the answering machine kicked in. I tried her cell. Turned off. I was a little baffled; I thought she had the day off, and she knew that today was my court hearing.

I tried Dorothea. She answered immediately, but sounded in a rush.

"Hello, Christine, I'll call you back later. I'm in a meeting at the moment, bye."

I was a little disappointed. She hadn't even asked how it went.

Edith couldn't hold back. *So where's this new life of yours? Not a peep from Richard, nor Luise or Dorothea. Great.*

I dialed Ines's number. Answering machine. Then Marleen. Her son answered the phone.

"Hello, it's Christine. Is your mother there?"

The annoyed voice of a seventeen-year-old answered me.

"Nah, Mom's gone shopping I think, no idea when she'll be back. Bye."

He hung up.

I was divorced and there was no one around to tell. My light feeling started to fade. Nina wasn't contactable, and Leonie had her answering machine on too.

I took a deep breath and lit up a cigarette.

At that moment my cell rang. Richard.

"It's me. Is it all done?"

"Richard. Yes, all over, it didn't even last half an hour."

"And how do you feel?"

"Good, but I'd really like to celebrate and can't get hold of anyone."

"Christine, I…"

Realizing he had misunderstood, I interrupted him. "I didn't mean you. Well, of course I did, but in particular my girlfriends in Hamburg. I can't get hold of any of them."

Richard's voice sounded a little relieved. "Oh, the girls will be in touch soon, I'm sure. I'm looking forward to Monday, very much."

Every time we spoke he caressed my soul. "I'm looking forward to it too. Until Monday then."

We hung up. I parked in front of my apartment. I went to the door, noticing the name sign next to my bell. Bernd's name. I had decided to take back my maiden name. I'd get a new sign made next week. Thinking about it gave me a nice feeling. I had no mail, no messages on my answering machine.

Edith voiced my fears. *No one's interested in your divorce. They're acting as if it were nothing more significant than a trip to the dentist. That's sad.*

Before my thoughts could go down the same path, the doorbell rang. I pressed the buzzer and Dorothea climbed up the stairs. She had a white rose in her hand.

"Miss Christine, you are now officially set free from your baggage. Congratulations."

I closed the door behind her and followed her into the kitchen.

"I could be coping really badly, you know. You can't congratulate someone on their divorce!"

I filled a narrow vase with water and put the rose in it. Dorothea sank down onto a chair and unbuttoned her coat. "But you're not coping badly. Why would you be? Just take a look at yourself. You never looked this good when you were a wife, your friends are more beautiful and much wittier, your bank account is fuller, and you're having better sex."

I sat opposite her. "What do you know about my sex life? And none of my witty friends have been in touch."

Dorothea laughed and buttoned her coat back up. "You always have better sex with lovers, like I do with Nils.

227

Anyway, I'm not stopping; I was coming by to pick you up. It's cocktail evening tonight in Café Wien. I got some vouchers from my mother, so we're going there and we're going to get drunk."

She stood up.

I groaned. "Dorothea, I only just got back, and I'm not really in the mood."

I felt like she wasn't taking me seriously.

She ignored my answer and took my jacket from the hall stand.

"Come on, put it on. I'm driving."

Reluctantly, I obeyed.

Dorothea found a space right in front of the bar. The café was lit with fairy lights, and the surface of the Alster was twinkling. I thought of Marleen and that first weekend when she had visited me when I was miserable. We had bought lingerie and drank Prosecco here. That had been one of the very first good days. Many, many more had come since then.

I smiled at Dorothea as she walked behind me. "You know, maybe this was a good idea. Perhaps people really should celebrate divorces."

"Not the divorces themselves, but their new life, yes."

I opened the entrance door and walked over to the first free table. Dorothea walked on by, which surprised me, but I followed her. I suddenly saw a long table filled with flowers and a champagne cooler. They were all there, raising their glasses. Luise, Leonie, Michael, Nina, Franziska, Ines, Georg, even Marleen.

I was speechless, and I just stared at them all. I couldn't say a word.

Dorothea pressed a glass into my hand and said to the others, "Don't worry, she's not silent because she's upset, she's just worried she has to pay for all this."

Multiple voices cried out in reproachful unison. "Dorothea!"

I started to laugh and hugged Ines, who had gotten up and was standing in front of me.

"It's so wonderful that you're all here. And I thought no one cared about my divorce."

Ines took a step back and looked at me. "So how was it?"

I thought about it. "Quick, strange, and painless. I'm just happy that that chapter is over."

Ines handed me a narrow package. "This is for you, so you've got it in writing too."

I unwrapped the paper. Nine pairs of eyes watched me. A door sign. My maiden name was inscribed in black, curving script on a silver background. I felt choked with emotion. Not grief, but a mixture of pride, thankfulness, and confidence.

Marleen stood up, raised her glass, and looked around the table, then at me.

"So, welcome back. Here's to your life never being peaceful and well-ordered again. I'm convinced that you will achieve everything you set out to do."

Dorothea popped the next champagne cork. I looked at the faces around me, at the lights that were lining the water's edge, at my new door sign, and then at my ring. I felt like I had arrived. And I felt very strong. Edith and Charlotte were in agreement for once.

Then I drank champagne.

About the Author

Author photo (c) Regina Geisler.

Dora Heldt was born on the North Sea island of Sylt, Germany. She works as a publisher's sales representative and currently lives in Hamburg. *Life After Forty* is the first of Heldt's bestsellers to be published in English.

About the Translator

Jamie Lee Searle is a freelance translator and reviewer of German language literature for publications such as *New Books in German*. She translates literary fiction, including short stories and texts by authors such as Feridun Zaimoglu and Ralf Rothmann, for publishing houses and cultural organizations throughout Europe and the U.S. She lives in London. In 2010, she cofounded the publishing collective *And Other Stories*, which seeks to promote and publish international literature in translation in the United Kingdom.